MW01280085

The Agent

By

Barbara M. Olson

www.barbaramolson.com
989-370-3732

Printed in the United States of America

Books by Barbara M. Olson

Cindy Lawton Series

The Inheritance
The Heir
The Cult
The Orphan
The Kidnapping
The Sisters
The Victim
The Corpse
The Storm

The Bertha Schlinkenmayer Series

The Agent
The Island [coming soon]

Dedication

To my niece

Rachael Joy Morrison, {July 28, 1983 – February 25, 2007}.

She was a beautiful Christian woman who wrote on her laptop just weeks before her tragic automobile accident. "I have been blessed. God has blessed me with so much and I can't begin to thank him enough." And we thank God for allowing us her love for twenty-three years.

Book One

The Agent

Characters

Bertha Schlinkenmayer
Jeff Schlinkenmayer {Bertha's late husband]
Elizabeth and Max Van Patten
{Bertha's daughter and son-in-law}
Eric Hoffermeister-R.V. companion
Budd and Hattie Hoffermeister
{Eric's father and mother}
Mary and Steve Lawral
{Eric's sister and brother-in-law}
Hazel and Carl Sanderson
{Eric's secretary and handyman husband}
Kathy Morrison {Eric's receptionist}
Annette {Bertha's Michigan friend}
Arthur Plant
Nancy Plant {Arthur's deceased wife}
Lizzie Plant {Arthur's sister}
Kurt Davis {former chief of police
in California and New Mexico}
Gary Hanraty {Local Chief of Police}
Ann Hanraty {Gary's wife}
Sally and Don Benjamin {Detectives}

Chapter One

As Bertha Schlinkenmayer drove her new R.V. into the campsite that night, she did so with a lot of apprehension. This would be the first time she had ever traveled alone. It had not been too bad during the day but she was not looking forward to the night. She was proud however that she had finally made a decision. She had merely existed since Jeff's death. It had been over two years and she found herself almost cut off from most of her married friends. She could not blame them; they all tried to make her feel comfortable. However, who needed a third dinner partner or card player?

Her daughter Liz and her husband, her late husband's son and wife, from a precious marriage, came with their three children to help her get through the funeral. Jeff had married his first wife when they were both relatively young. They only had one child. His first wife died after a short illness leaving, Jeff with a small son to care for alone.

Bertha met Jeff and they married and enjoyed a good life together. They loved one another dearly right up until his death. Jeff died of a heart attack. He was only fifty-two years old

7

and never been sick a day. The attack hit him as he drove home after a very productive meeting, with a group of salespeople from his Real Estate office.   He must have realized something was wrong. The police said it looked like he pulled his Town Car over to the curb and died. They found him slumped over the wheel. It was so like Jeff; if he thought there was something wrong he would pull over instead of trying to get to a hospital for fear he might harm someone if he lost consciousness. Bertha could not help but wonder why he had not called her on the cell phone. She concluded the crummy thing was probably out of juice again. She had asked him a number of times to get a new one but he never seemed to have the time. She had purchased one for him for Christmas and put away until the Holidays.

The new cell phone remained wrapped in Christmas paper in Bertha's closet for over two years until she took it out of its wrappings and decided to have it installed in the R.V., after she purchased her little rig. She was ready for her trip the following week after she took it in for service to make it ready for her journey to Michigan.

Bert stood in front of the mirror in her little travel bus, and brushed a stray blond hair from her right cheek. She had been completely white-haired since her daughter's birth. Jeff had loved her white crop. He used to kid her and tell her to leave it as it was because he did not want people to know he had robbed the cradle. She never felt she was that much younger then he. Whenever her daughter Liz got into trouble, Jeff would tease their daughter by telling her she had made her mother's hair turn white over night. Sometimes Bertha thought, when Liz was in grade school, she was a little embarrassed her mother's hair was so white. All her friend's mothers were either blond or brunets, but Liz never told her she wanted her to color it so she had not done so. She was going to get a shock when her mother arrived at her front door.

I needed to do something to make me feel better; hadn't Liz suggested that when she was at the funeral, she said to herself. She had been feeling so old, now that she was a widow. She went to the phone and made an appointment at her hairdressers. Her beautician yelled so loud, when she told her she wanted to color her hair that Bert laughed for the first time since Jeff's death. The women had been trying for years to get her to color her hair. The little beautician told her she would work her in that afternoon. She was not going to take a chance Bert might change her mind. Bert dropped off the R.V. and told the man he could keep the rig for several hours. She would pick it up after her hair appointment. She walked to the restaurant and ordered a large salad. She had over an hour before her appointment so she did a little shopping and then headed for the salon.

Bertha would miss her home and neighbors, but was surprised she felt little remorse selling the house and most of her furnishings. She put what remained into storage. No one seemed to pay too much attention to her hair as she said her goodbyes at her going-away party. The next morning she pulled out of her drive for the last time. Oh, Sylvia her closest neighbor, had made a fuss over her hair. She said Bert should have done it years before. Bert knew she was trying to make light of her leaving and wanted Bertha to leave with a good laugh. They hugged one another, promising to write and then Bert was off for Michigan.

The decision to keep dying her hair was still open. So many older women tried to look younger with blond hair. After a few months, if she started to look like some of them, it would be back to white hair.

Chapter Two

Well girl, she said to herself as she walked from the R. V. that night, time to go face the public. She went behind the rig and opened the side panel to remove the electrical cord. She was bending over looking for the plug for the T.V. when a man who looked to be in his thirties, walked over and offered to help. "Are you traveling alone?" he questioned.

"Yes! I lost my husband and I'm headed for my daughter's home in Michigan," she said and then wondered why she was telling the young man her personal itinerary.

"Wow!" He said. "That is quite a long way to go it alone."

"You look like you are traveling alone," she commented.

"Yes, but I'm not an attractive, defenseless, young lady," he smiled.

She laughed and said, "I'm not as defenseless as you might think and I am far from being young. You're probably young enough to date my daughter," she snapped.

"I guess I better go back to my rig and study up on my manners. I don't seem to be doing too well." He smiled a beautiful smile and walked away.

Smiling, Bertha thought she had just met her first flirt since leaving home. She wondered how many more would be out there. Actually, he seemed like a nice enough young man. She could have taken some of the sharpness out of her voice. She would have to stop being so defensive. It was a dead give-away to her uncertainty.

As she was about to prepare a light meal, a knock came at her door. The young man was standing there with a flower. "I'd like to try again, to introduce myself; I am Eric Hoffermeister. Single, never married and have a knack for saying the wrong thing." He bowed his head and added. "I would like to take you to dinner. Now, you can slam the door in my face or accept my inept invitation," He handed her a rose and gave her that beautiful smile again.

She laughed and accepted the flower. "With our last names, no one will ever forget us." She told him and introduced herself. "I don't know how you knew roses are my favorite flower. I could not very well refuse such a humble invitation to dinner. Would you want to take my rig; it is far easier to park?"

"I wouldn't think of it. I have my chariot waiting for you," He smiled.

She looked around behind him as he moved to one side. He had removed his scooter from the back of his R.V. and had it parked behind her door. "Will it hold us both?" she questioned.

"You look so light; it won't even know you're behind me," he smiled. "Here!" he said and handed her a helmet, "You should always wear a helmet regardless of a bike's size. She hated to put it on her new hair-do but he helped her strap on the helmet and the two climbed up onto the scooter. Eric turned the throttle with his right hand; the little bike gently pulled forward. Bert was surprised she enjoyed the air in her face. It had been a long time since she was on such a small size motor bike. This must be why dogs always stick there noses out the window when they ride in a car, she thought; the air smells so crisp and pure. She would have to get herself one of these bikes. She would not have to unhook whenever she wanted to go somewhere. She mentioned the fact at dinner and Eric offered to help her pick one out at the local dealer.

The next day he was over to her R.V. bright and early. "I didn't know if you wanted to go to the dealer this morning. I thought you could drive your rig and I'll lead the way on my scooter. I went there and purchased a new light earlier today. He has several similar bikes on his display floor," He told her.

"Thank you. Give me about five minutes and I'll come by your R.V. and honk when I'm ready," She told him.

She hurriedly combed her hair, applied some lipstick, got behind her wheel, and was at his R.V. in exactly five minutes.

He smiled when he came out and said, "Are you always on time?"

"No, sometimes I'm early," she smiled back at him.

The cycle shop was only ten minutes away from the park. She pulled up along side his scooter and got out.

"Let me do the talking," he said. "This guy likes to dicker and I know what the bike should cost you. I would suggest you purchase this year's model and get the next step up from mine. I wish now I had one with a little more power."

"I'll be happy to let you lead. I have no idea what one of these things is worth. I would like an aqua blue one to match my rig, if that's possible," she said and followed him into the building.

Several minutes later, the owner walked over and asked if he could be of help. "I hope so. This lady would like to purchase one of your bikes, if they are not too expensive. That red one looks nice," Eric said. He knew she wanted the aqua one but did not want to seem too interested. He also knew that the aqua one would not be as easy to sell. They might get a good price if the shop owner did not know that was the one she really wanted.

"This one is a little expensive. It is our most popular model," the salesman said. "I can give you a better deal on one of the other bikes."

"Just tell us how much this one will cost," Eric said and ran his hand over the front fender.

The man quoted him a price and then added, "But, I can give you this one for three hundred less and I'll even throw in a horn. I'll tell you what; I'll even throw in a matching helmet," he said pointing to the aqua bike.

Eric looked at Bertha. "What is wrong with it?" Bertha asked.

"Nothing, I assure you Ma'am. This is actually a better bike than the red one, but for some reason the color doesn't move. It has been on my floor longer than any other bike. I could sell six red ones at full price, if I got rid of it."

"If she purchases the aqua bike; how much for a carrier that fits on the back of her rig?" Eric asked.

"For you, a hundred bucks," the owner said.

"Make it seventy-five, the matching helmet and the horn and I'll take the aqua one," Bert said.

Eric looked at her and smiled. He knew the guy would take eighty but seventy-five would make him think about turning down her offer.

"You sure negotiate a hard bargain lady," the man said but he started writing up the sales slip. "It will take me about an hour to put the proper hitch on your rig and install the bike securely."

"There is a small diner at the end of this street. Why don't we go get some coffee," Eric suggested as he walked toward the door.

"Fine; give me a moment to finish writing this check and I'll be right with you," Bert told him.

After they were outside, Eric said, "I don't know that I would have paid him before he finished installing the scooter onto your rig."

"I paid him so he would not come up with any hidden charges or sell it to the next guy that offered him a few more bucks for it," she smiled.

"Yeah, It would be just like him," Eric laughed.

They walked side by side to the diner and Eric held the door open for Bert. When she entered, she smelled the heavenly aroma of fresh baked rolls. "Oh my, I think I may have to forgo my diet and have one of those wonderful smelling rolls," Bert said.

"Diet; now why would you be on a diet?" Eric asked.

"Ha! Flattery will only buy you a roll," she laughed. "I have to watch everything I eat or the pounds pile on me. Now what roll would you like? This is my treat, and I don't want any arguments. You have been far too kind, introducing me to the scooter craze," Bertha smiled and pointed to the roll she wanted in the display cabinet. "I think I want the Bear Claw. Is it one of those that you don't cook in fat?" she asked the clerk.

"Why, yes Ma'am. Most people don't know that until I tell them," The clerk said.

"There was a small bakery near our home in California that carried them and we used to buy one after church on Sunday and call it our lunch," Bert told the young lady.

"I'll have one too, please," Eric said and the lady smiled at the nice couple.

"She thought you were talking about us," Eric smiled. "See, she didn't think you were old enough to have a daughter for me to date," he teased.

Bertha ignored him and he laughed.

When they returned to the dealer, there was a lovely aqua scooter on the back bumper of her rig. The owner came out to greet them, carrying her aqua helmet, and said, "That hitch costs a little more than I thought."

She merely smiled, thanked him, took the helmet, told him what a nice job he had done for her, and started to get into her R.V. Eric said, "I'll meet you back at camp."

"I told you, I am expected at my brothers in Arizona for dinner so I have to be leaving. Thank you again for your kindness. I hope we meet again sometime in our travels," she said and meant it.

"You never know, and thank you for the wonderful company. It has been a pleasant couple days," he answered and took her out stretched hand and squeezed it. She drove off still feeling the warmth of his grip.

Chapter Three

Bertha arrived at her brother's home and enjoyed him and his wife's company for two days. They took her out to dinner at their favorite restaurants and her sister-in-law took her shopping for more turquoise jewelry. Turquoise jewelry was Bertha's favorite. She had been collecting it for years and it was hard to find the little corn shaped pieces. She was lucky enough to find a matching pair of earrings that was going to be lovely with the necklace Jeff had bought her on their last trip to Prescott, Arizona. She spotted a delicate little bracelet in the squash pattern and purchased it as well. As she started to leave the shop, she spotted a lovely turquoise ring and had to have it. Her sister-in-law laughed and the owner smiled as he wrote out another bill of sale.

Her brother and sister-in-law were very nice people, but it was not the same visiting them alone. Oh well! She had better get used to it.

She pulled out of Sedona three days later and headed east on highway 40 toward Branson, Missouri. Before leaving Arizona, she called and made reservations for a campsite near the main street so she would not have too far to go to enjoy the shows. She arrived two days later and pulled up to the lovely campsite they assigned her; a space right on the bank over looking a lake. She could feel the tension ease from her body. She would do some fishing the next day and maybe catch her dinner. She climbed from her rig. She put out the awning and installed the little screen porch to it. She had her rig set for a two or three day stay in less than thirty minutes. She was getting pretty good at it and smiled to herself.

She dressed in clean jeans, shirt and jacket and went out of the rig to her new bike. It was relatively easy getting it off the small ramp. The ramp dropped down and she wheeled it to the ground. She forgot her helmet and had to go back inside for it. She was not about to ride without it. She put on the helmet, mounted the bike and pushed the start button. The little bike hummed. I'm going to like this, she said to herself; I also have to stop talking to myself, she laughed.

She was just in time to see the show. This was the third time she had seen the family show. The kids were all adults now and so talented. She could not believe what the eldest daughter could do with a violin. She was not a fan of violin music, but she was a fan of this young lady. She bought one of cassettes and left for the camp.

On the way, she stopped and got a cappuccino in a Styrofoam cup with a lid and balanced it on the carrier, taking it back to her rig. She dismounted, set the cappuccino on the step, and then chained the bike to the rear bumper. There was no sense putting it back on the rack.

She planned to stay a couple days. She had tickets for the showboat dinner theater the following evening and tickets during the day for a comedian's show she had wanted to see. They say the lady's room at his theater was worth the price of admission. The managers of the park were most helpful and were able to get her a seat at the captain's table on the cruise. They also got her an aisle seat at the comedians for the afternoon show. She picked up her cappuccino and entered her rig. She would watch some T.V. and catch up on the latest news before retiring. She did not finish her drink but fell asleep half way through the news report. She must have been far more tired from the trip then she realized. When she awoke, she noted she had not even made up her bed. She had put on her P.J.'s before watching the boob tube, but made the mistake of lying down before pulling the bed together, and had already slept half the night. She pulled the afghan around her and went back to sleep.

The following morning was misty and spotted with rain showers. She went to the front office and asked when the trolleys would be running. The owner offered to drive her into town as he had errands to run and would have his wife pick her up after the show. The trolley was not going to stop anywhere near the show she wanted to see. She told him she would just take her rig if the weather stayed wet. His wife insisted she allow them to take her there and back. Bertha finally agreed, "But only if it keeps raining," she smiled and left their office.

As luck would have it, the sun came out and it turned out to be a lovely day. She got in a little fishing but was unable to catch anything worth keeping. She put her gear away and went in to clean up before leaving for town.

Bertha came out, got on her bike and went into town for the afternoon show. Parking her scooter out in front, she chained it to a pipe and went into the show. It was hilarious. The star asked for jokes from the audience and like a fool, she raised her hand. She did not know what had gotten into her. They had five other people telling jokes and then the comedian said he wanted everyone to applaud for their favorite; the winner was to go up on stage and M.C. the program with the comedian. The women next to Bert said she was going to win. Bertha smiled but hoped she was wrong. The women did everything she could to keep the applause meter going and sure enough, Bertha found she was up on stage. To her surprise, she was not nervous. The comedian was very nice and easy to talk to. The interview got a lot of laughs and everyone seemed to enjoy it. During intermission, several people came up and told her what a grand job she had done. Bertha was happy when the show was over. She received a tape of her part in the show and wanted to get home and play it. She had no idea what she had done or said in those ten minutes. She just hoped she had not made too big a fool of herself. She reminded herself not to tell any more jokes when asked by the star of a show.

As she was unlocking her bike a voice behind her said, "Hello, I didn't know you were such a star." It was Eric, standing over her.

"How did you get here?" she asked.

"I came for the shows. You can't believe how surprised I was when I saw you go up on the stage. You were great. I don't think I would have been that calm," he told her.

"He made it easy. Now what are you doing here; following me?" she said.

"No, I just thought it was a good idea to see some shows. I've been here for a week. There isn't much I haven't seen. What is your next stop?" he asked.

She told him, "I'm going on the showboat tonight. They say the food is good and the show is excellent."

"I didn't see that one. I didn't want to go alone. It didn't seem right," He said. "I wonder if I can still get tickets. That is if you don't mind."

"You can try but I imagine the regular tickets are sold out. I am at the captains' table. There is usually a few left; they are a little high priced," she told him.

He took out his cell phone and before she had her helmet on, he had purchased a ticket and talked the women on the other end of the line to seat him next to Bertha.

"I got a ticket," he smiled at her. "May I pick you up? There is no sense in both of us driving."

"I'll pick you up. I'm quite a way out of town. I want to show off how well I handle my new bike anyway. Where are you staying?"

"The same place you are if they have a vacancy. I checked out of my place earlier in the day and I'm looking for another campsite. A bunch of kids moved in last night and partied all night. I didn't get any sleep."

Bert laughed and said, "I'm sure they have a site. Do you want to follow me?"

"Sure. Lead the way," he smiled and went out behind the theater and got his rig.

He followed her back to her camp and was able to rent the site next to hers. It had been vacated earlier in the day. "This is convenient," he smiled at her.

"Now we won't have to wait for one another to be picked up," she smiled, but knew he meant more. She made up her mind to leave the next day. She could still remember the warmth of his hand and there was no way she would permit it to go any farther.

That night on the showboat, she had to admit was the nicest time she had spent since Jeff's death. The show was as advertised. The ventriloquist and his dog were great. He had the cutest talking dog, and threw his voice into the dog. The dog sat so still you could not tell he was real until the handler took him off the stage. The ventriloquist had an apparatus around the dog's neck and he moved it up and down. It looked like the dog was moving his mouth. It was quite a show. The meal was palatable and desert very fattening. They did a lot of laughing and were still talking about the show the following morning as they enjoyed coffee in the small room off the office the owners used for a gathering place.

"I have to get packed up and on the road before too long," She said. "I don't want to get in the morning traffic in Indianapolis. I plan to get as far as possible tonight." She knew she was rambling again but did not want to hear any arguments from him. She wanted to get away from him as soon as possible.

"Yes! I have to leave too. My brother in Gaylord expects me in three days so that means a lot of driving and little sight-seeing," Eric said.

"I guess it does. It always took Jeff and me a day and a half after we got into Michigan to get to Gaylord. You can do it in a day but only if you're already in Michigan and want to drive straight through," she said.

"You know where Gaylord is?" Eric smiled. "I had no idea where it was located until I got a map from my brother. He told me to go through Lansing and on up," Eric told her.

"He's right. It will be a nice trip. It is all express-way," she told him but did not mention she still owned a home outside of Gaylord.

They followed each other by about two hours. She went out first, drove most of the day, and found a campsite outside of Terra Haute. The next day she was on the road by six o'clock. Surprised she was able to get up so early. She quickly packed up and pulled out of the site. She had driven so far the day before, she was pleased to see she could get through Indianapolis by following route 70 instead of taking the BI-pass and got onto route 69 heading for Marshall, Michigan. She continued and picked up 94 toward Plymouth. It had been so long since she drove to Michigan; she hoped she was taking the shortest route to her daughters.

Chapter Four

Bertha was in town before three o'clock that afternoon. Her daughter would not get out of work until four-thirty so she went downtown to her bookstore. When she walked in her daughter was ringing up a sale. She stayed in the background until she finished. Bert walked over and put a book on the counter before her daughter. Her head was down and when she saw the book she said, "You'll love this; my mother wrote it." Looking up she saw her mother and said, "Mom, you're here already. I wanted to get home and clean house a little before you arrived."

Bertha did not tell her why she cut her Branson trip short. "I can imagine you might have a speck of dirt somewhere if we really look hard," she smiled. "I can go leave and come back later," Bertha offered.

"Not on your life," she said and called one of her clerks asking her to take over and close up that night. She was going to take her mother and go home. She quickly introduced Bertha to the two clerks and the mother and daughter walked arm and arm out the back door of the shop. "Where is your car?" Elizabeth asked.

"I sold it. There is my transportation," she told her, pointing to her R.V.

"Mother! You didn't drive that thing all the way from California," she exclaimed.

"I'm afraid I did," Bertha laughed, "and I had a ball. It is the only way to travel."

"We'll talk about it when we get home. If you follow me, I'll lead you out of town. We are about a mile out, off Ann Arbor Trail."

"Isn't that where dad and I had a place; in Colony Farms?" she asked.

"Yes. If we lose contact; I'll meet you at the Colony Farm entrance," Elizabeth smiled.

They had no trouble following one another and when her daughter pulled up into a driveway, no one could have been more surprised than Bertha.

Jumping from her rig she exclaimed, "You bought our old home. You didn't tell me."

"I wanted to surprise you," her daughter laughed.

"Well you did," Bertha smiled. "Let's go in. I can't wait to see what you've done to the inside."

The two women went to the front door. "You have to see it from the main door first. Next time you can come in through the garage," Elizabeth smiled.

Elizabeth unlocked the door and stood to one side so Bertha could walk in.

The first thing Bertha saw was the beautiful natural oak, open, curved staircase. She looked to her right and saw a blue and white living room. "It looks just like we left it," Bertha said.

"I tried to re-do it, as much as I could remember. I wanted it to look like our home where I grew up. It always felt so warm and inviting," Elizabeth said.

"I didn't realize you loved it so much," Bertha said.

"Mom! I had some of my most wonderful years here. You can't imagine how I felt when Max was transferred to Michigan and I found out we could move to Plymouth." She told her.

"Probably as happy as I was when we owned the house. Now you know how I must have really felt when I learned we had to move to California," Bert remarked.

"But Mom, you had some of your best years there. I've heard you say so many times," her daughter told her.

"Yes, you're right, but you didn't see the tears I shed, when I first heard your father wanted to move clear across the country," Bert smiled.

"Well, come on. The best is yet to come," Elizabeth told her and took her hand, walking to the right wing of the large home. "Close your eyes," she told her Mom.

Bertha smiled and closed them. She waited until her daughter told her to open them and when she did, she could not believe what she saw. There set a huge oak, cannon ball, king sized bedroom suite. It looked just like the one she had purchased many years ago for this room.

Bertha almost cried. "Where did you find this set?" she exclaimed.

"I told you we wanted you to stay. It only came last week. We had to order it from your favorite Plymouth furniture store. He was so kind and patient. You would have thought it was still grandpa's store. He even gave us a break in the price. Do you really like it? We want you to be comfortable," Elizabeth said.

"It is lovely dear, but I told you; I am not moving in with you," Bert told her. "It is kind of you and Max to ask me, but I don't want to live with anyone right now. This should be your and Max's room. I'll be very comfortable upstairs in a guestroom."

Max walked in the side door and hollered, "Where is my lovely mother?" He never called her his mother-in-law and it got a little confusing sometimes if his real mother was in the room, but Bertha loved having him feel close enough to call her mother.

"We are in Mom's room," Elizabeth yelled back and when he walked in, he gave Bertha a big hug.

He stepped back and said, "I like it."

She knew he was talking about her hair. Her daughter had not even mentioned it. Evidently, she did not like it.

"Mother refuses to live with us," Elizabeth pouted.

"I told her you wouldn't," Max told Bert. "I can't say I blame you, but you know there will be a day when you might need too; if that time ever arrives we expect you to stay with us."

"That is sweet of you. I'll keep that in mind," Bert smiled. "Now show me the rest of the house."

They toured the house and Elizabeth suggested they go out to Bert's favorite restaurant for dinner. Bertha knew her daughter did not enjoy cooking so she readily agreed. Bert would be glad to get up north to her home in Michaywe'. As much as she enjoyed her little R.V., she was getting a little tired of cooking in it, or eating in restaurants.

They enjoyed a quiet dinner and Bert had her favorite, Eggplant Lasagna. "You won't believe this but with all the great restaurants in California; I have not been able to find Eggplant Lasagna like they make right here in Plymouth," She told them.

During dinner, she broke the news to her daughter. "I am going up north and opening up the house tomorrow," she announced.

"Mother, you can't do that. You just got here. I can't get off for at least a week. You're going to need our help," Elizabeth told her.

"I won't need any help. Many of our friends are still living there and if they are busy, I can hire any help I might need." Bert told her.

"Mother, I won't have it. You can wait until I can get away." She told her.

Max could see the two headstrong women were at a standstill. "I have an idea," he said. "I don't have to be at work for at least another week. I have everything caught up and my staff will be glad to see me take some time off. Mom, why don't I go with you? Elizabeth can pick me up when she can get away. That way you will have help and Liz can stop worrying." He wanted to say she could stop trying to mother her mother.

Max knew why Bert did not want to live with them and he could not blame her.

"That's a wonderful idea, dear," Elizabeth said. "Max, if you're sure you can take the time, I would love the company," Bert smiled at her son-in-law. She would enjoy his company. She had not been looking forward to arriving there alone.

Chapter Five

The next day found Max driving Bertha's new R.V. and heading for Gaylord. "I can't believe how easily your rig handles. I can see why you enjoyed the trip from California. Never having to worry about a room or dragging everything in at night and out in the morning," he smiled at her. "I'd buy one of these in a heartbeat if I could get Elizabeth to travel in it. Maybe while she is here you could talk to her and tell her how convenient you found it."

Bertha smiled, "I'll try but I think we will be wasting our time," she laughed.

"It was too bad you couldn't visit Jeff Jr. and Marie but they still have another year in Europe before he can return home," Max said.

"Yes, but he is making a great deal of money and seems to enjoy the travel. It is good she has the three children. When the kids aren't in school they go everywhere with him. We talk at least twice a month and he fills me in on the places and things they have seen," Bertha told Max. "He finally sold his home here and after purchasing a flat in London they were happy they no longer had two payments to pay and the house was off their back.

"Yeah, in a way, I envy them. They will have some great memories," he smiled at her. "Can you imagine the places and things those kids are experiencing. They are seeing things few of us ever get to see."

The trip was lovely. The trees were all in full leaf and the roadwork was close to completion so there were few delays. They arrived at Bert's home early in the afternoon and had plenty of daylight left to get inside and turn everything on. Luckily, there were no busted pipes or fuses blown. It was a very smooth house opening

Bertha went over and turned on the fireplace. A warm glow filled the room. "I am so happy we never got rid of this place. We always enjoyed it so much and could not wait to visit whenever possible. We wanted to spend a Christmas here the year he died. Looks like I'll be doing it alone unless you and Elizabeth will join me," she said.

"Of course we will be here but are you going to fly in or drive here from California?" Max asked.

"I didn't tell Elizabeth but I will be staying here. I sold my home in California and plan on taking permanent residence here," Bertha told him.

"You're kidding; that's great. What did you do with all the furniture and cars?" he asked.

"I sold almost everything I didn't want to keep. The remainder of the things went to the family that purchased the house. I did save some keepsakes that I put in storage. I will call the Storage Company and they will send my things here, as soon as I get settled," she smiled at her son-in-law.

Max's jaw had dropped when she told him she was here for good and his mouth was still open. He never knew his Mom-in-law could be so well organized. "Elizabeth is going to have a Hairy Fit," he laughed. "I can't wait until you tell her. Well! Let's go to the clubhouse for dinner. I am starved. I am not used to this much physical work. I could not believe all we brought in from your R.V."

"It is a fooler isn't it. I had room for more but thought I'd have the rest sent. I was afraid I would wear down the tires if I overloaded it," Bertha laughed. "Let me put on a fresh face and blouse and we will go to dinner," she said as she walked from the living room, down the hall and into the left wing of the house. Her room was just as she left it on their last trip. She was glad she had changed the sheets before they had left. She didn't want to smell Jeff's after-shave lotion. She slept in their bed in California for four nights after his death and cried every time she rolled over to his side of the bed and smelled his familiar scent. She finally laundered everything in the house he had touched and her loss was a little easier to handle.

"Hey! What is taking so long," Max yelled from the kitchen. "Remember; I get mean when I get hungry. I didn't see anything wrong with you before."

Bertha laughed. She always told them she was the one that got mean when she got hungry. She quickly changed her blouse and went into the kitchen to find Max finishing a soft drink.

"Well come on," she said. "I don't want you telling my daughter I starved you to death."

He helped her into her jacket and they left the house.

Chapter Six

The clubhouse restaurant was humming. They would have to wait twenty minutes to be seated. "Would you like to go into town?" Max asked.

"No, let's sit at the bar and have some wine, while we wait," Bert suggested.

"This I got to see," he teased. "I don't think I've seen you take more than one glass of wine even at Christmas," He laughed.

They sat there for only a few minutes when a voice behind her said, Schlick, is that you?" She knew immediately it was Eric. He had started calling her Schlick right after she purchased the scooter and talked the man down in price.

"Eric! What in the world are you doing here?" Bert asked.

"I told you my sister had a place in Gaylord, remember?" he said.

Max was looking at the handsome man talking to his mother-in-law. He did not know why he was so surprised he looked enamored with Bertha. It would be impossible not to hit on her. After all, she was attractive and single. It was bound to happen sometime.

"Excuse me Eric, this is Max Van Patten. Max this is Eric Hoffermeister. We met at one of the campsites coming across country from California," Bertha said, introducing the two men.

He acknowledged the introduction and said, "I'm here with my sis and brother-in-law. Why don't you join us? We can move in a couple more chairs and you won't have to wait for a table. We were about to order," Eric said.

Bertha looked at Max, who said, "Mother and I would love to join you."

Bert smiled; Max usually called her Bert when they were out in public.

They walked into the main dining room and Eric introduced them to his sister Mary and her husband Steve.

"Are you Bertha Schlinkenmayer!" she bubbled. "I thought he had made you up. It is so nice to meet you. Eric said he enjoyed the trip here because he had such good company," she smiled at Bertha.

Bert knew she would have some explaining to do when she and Max got back to the house and tried to change the subject.

"Where do you live in Gaylord?" Bert asked her.

"Right here in Michaywe. We built a house here about five years ago and just recently decided to move here permanently," Steve told her. "I do free lance writing and can work almost anywhere. Mary is an R.N. so she can always find work."

"How nice it would have been to be able to move to Gaylord when we were young enough to enjoy it. My husband, Jeff and I never got the opportunity. He was transferred around so much, but this was always home base. We built a new home about the same time you did, in hopes of retiring here. It was the second house we built in Michaywe. I guess I will have to retire here by myself," Bert told them.

"Are you going to stay in Gaylord?" Mary asked.

"Yes, in Michaywe. I have had enough of California. If I want warm weather, I'll go to Florida and see my sister. This winter she and her husband asked me to come down for several weeks," Bert told her.

"I think that is wonderful. Now maybe I can get Eric to spend more time here," she smiled.

The waitress interrupted before Bert could comment. They ordered and enjoyed a fine meal. Bertha looked at her watch and was surprised they had taken two hours for dinner. The new couple was easy to talk to and very interesting. Steve was thrilled to find another writer in the area. She finally excused herself and Max and she left for home.

Max did not mention Eric until they were seated in the living room watching the late news.

"Well young woman, are you going to explain yourself and Eric?" Max asked.

"You sound like Elizabeth," she told him.

"Don't try to wiggle out of it. Where did you meet him? He seemed very smitten with you," Max said.

"What an old fashioned word, smitten," she smiled.

"Don't try to change the subject Bert, fess-up," Max insisted.

She explained by telling him about her trip from California again, but this time she included the part Eric played.

"Great! It sounds like you were very fortunate to meet such a nice friend," Max told her. "I hope you plan on seeing more of him. I liked him."

"Good heavens Max; He is at least eight years younger then I am," Bert told him.

"So, I'm eight and a half years older then Elizabeth," he said.

"That's different," Bertha insisted.

"I don't see why," Max told her. "You could do worse. I'm not saying you should marry him and I can't see why you were so upset that I accepted their invitation for cocktails Saturday evening. We were going to dinner at the club anyway."

"It's done now, but what if Elizabeth shows up early. What will she say?" Bert said.

"She told us she won't be here till the middle of next week, so don't worry about it. If she does, I'll handle her. It is none of her business who you see or don't see. You are going to have to understand, mother. She won't like anyone you decide to date."

"I haven't decided to date anyone," Bert insisted.

"It sounds like you already have," Max laughed.

"Oh, go to bed," Bertha said, treating him like one of her children.

"Okay mama," He laughed, and walked over and kissed her on the forehead. "Sweet dreams," he added as he walked out of the room before she could swat at him.

She did have sweet dreams that night and felt very rested when she got up the next morning.

Chapter Seven

Mary and Steve's home was a lovely chalet located only a few blocks from Bertha. They met Bert and Max at the door and welcomed them in for snacks. There were three other couples in attendance. "I hope you don't mind more company. I let it slip you were in town and they invited themselves."

Bertha walked in to find she knew the six people standing at the bar. "How nice to see you all," she said.

"You didn't tell us you were in residence, you stinker. What did you do to your hair; I love it." Grace said before Bertha had time to answer. She gave Bert a big hug and smiled as her husband Dan took Bert in his arms and kissed her cheek.

"We're so pleased you are back," Dan told her. "We were so sorry to hear about Jeff. We have all been contemplating what you would do now. We hope you plan on spending more time here."

"Well, I plan on staying in Michaywe' all year and making my permanent residence here," Bert told him.

"Wonderful," Charlotte yelled. "We can get our bridge club going again. I'm afraid we haven't been playing much since you left last year." Her husband smiled and gave Bert a peck on the cheek.

Betty and her husband agreed with Charlotte and everyone seemed happy to see her back.

At six o'clock Steve announced last call. "We are to be at the clubhouse by six thirty. I made reservations for eleven people."

Bert thought to herself, there is always going to be an odd number if I am included in the group again. It made her a little sad. To her surprise, she was not the odd man out; Max was. Eric took her arm and escorted her out to his sister's car.

"Come on Max, I'll drive," he told him. "I borrowed sis's car," he told Bertha, holding the door open for her. She quietly entered the car. She did not want to insist Max drive; it might cause a scene in front of her friends.

At dinner, Bert and Eric were seated next to each other, of course. Mary saw to that. She had Max seated at the end of the table so Bertha was between the two men. Steve and Mary sat opposite them and the others took the remaining seats around the table.

Everyone seemed to be talking at once and Bertha found it difficult to hear all the conversations. She managed to answer whenever anyone asked her a direct question but avoided telling them anything about Eric and her trip from California. They were all surprised she had come such a long way in an R.V. all by herself.

Bertha would be happy when the evening ended. She was more tired from her trip than she thought. It had been several days and she still had not gotten her strength back. She would stop at the health food store tomorrow and get some Siberian Ginseng. She knew that would help. She had run out before she headed north and should have purchased some in Plymouth before she started out again.

They had just ordered when a man entered the room. He was trying to throw his weight around and demanding he be seated immediately. "I made a reservation and you better have a table for me in four minutes," he snapped at the little hostess.

"I didn't know Arthur and Nancy Plant were still here. I wrote to Nancy at the address she had given me and the letter came back; not at this address. I was surprised because always before the address had been correct. I assumed they had moved and I would hear from her after she was settled. Who is that with him?" Bertha said.

"She is just one of his many young girl friends. Didn't you know; Nancy committed suicide a year ago," Mary told her.

"No! I don't believe it; but it is no wonder, being married to him. He was always knocking her around when I knew them. How did she do it?"

"That's what was so strange," Grace said. "She slit her throat."

"Now, I'm sure she didn't commit suicide. She wouldn't have done such a thing. She was too vain about her looks. She had been a model when he met her," Bert said.

"That was what the rest of us thought but the police said it was suicide. After her death, the ladies Wednesday afternoon bridge group kind of fell apart," Grace told her.

Before they were finished with their meal, Arthur stopped by their table.

"Bertha, I hardly recognized you. It is so nice to see you; love the hair. Are you going to be around for awhile?" Arthur asked.

"I am going to take up permanent residence here," Bert told him. She would not smile at him.

"Now that you are single, maybe we could see one another," he said.

"I'm afraid I will be very busy," she said, dismissing him. He took the hint and left for his own table. She did not want to be rude to anyone, but he always made her feel uncomfortable.

After dinner, everyone went back to his or her own homes. Eric took Max over to pick up their car after first dropping Bert off. "I'd like to have lunch later this week, if it is convenient," Eric told her before she exited his sister's car.

"You have my number," she said and smiled over her shoulder after she opened her front door.

Twenty minutes later Max came home. "That took long enough. Did you find out what you wanted to know," Bertha smiled at her son-in-law.

"I only asked him about his job. Did you know he has a private detective agency out west?" Max asked.

"He has several agencies from what I understand," Bert told him. "He never mentioned they were detective agencies."

"Yes! He wants to open another one here in the east," Max told her.

Bert smiled, "Why do the people in California always refer to us as, back east?" she questioned.

"Who knows, but I do wonder if he wanted the new office before or after he met my mother-in-law," Max pondered.

"That is enough of that. I told you I am too old for him and even if I weren't I am not ready to get into a relationship," she told him.

"I didn't notice anyone else tonight thinking he was too young for you," Max smiled.

"Let's change the subject, shall we. Elizabeth was on the answering service when I got home. She will be here sometime tomorrow. She plans to stay a few days so let's not mention Eric. It will only upset her."

"Mother I told you before, it is none of her business when or if you start seeing another man. You are too young to go on much longer alone. I know Jeff wouldn't want that," Max scolded.

"Thank you dear, but I feel pretty old at times. Right now, I am bushed and I'm headed for bed. See you in the morning," Bert said and left for her room.

She was tired when she crawled between the sheets, but her mind refused to stop racing for over an hour before she fell asleep from sheer exhaustion.

Elizabeth arrived the next afternoon and Bert suggested they all go into town for dinner. "Max and I have been eating every night at the club and I for one would like a change of menu," she said.

Max smiled at her. He wondered if she was afraid they might run into Eric but he didn't mention it and suggested they go for Chinese.

The next day Max and Elizabeth went north to Mackinaw Island to spend a day and night at an Inn Bert had told them about. She was waving goodbye to her daughter and son-in-law when the phone rang. She knew who it was before she picked it up.

"Hi Schlick! Would you and your family join Mary, Steve and I tonight for cocktails and dinner?" Eric asked.

"I'm afraid not. They just left for Mackinaw Island. They won't be back till late tomorrow and plan on leaving early the following morning, but thank you for asking," Bert said.

"All right then my second choice would be you're having lunch with me today. I hate to eat alone and Mary and Steve are golfing," Eric told her.

"I thought you golfed," Bert said.

"I do. I can pick you up about one o'clock, if that is convenient," Eric told her.

She hesitated for several seconds thinking, what if she runs into someone she knows? What would they think? But then, so what, she was only having lunch. "I'll be ready," she heard herself say. Like a teenager, she started thinking about what she would wear as soon as she hung up the phone.

They were finishing their main course when Eric asked, "My sister wants me to ask you all over before they leave again. We thought we would have drinks at the house and go to the club for dinner. What do you think; will they come?"

"I don't know why not. They have to eat sometime. Max and you get along so well; I am sure he would like to say goodbye to you and your family."

"Do you have time for a movie? There is one starting in about twenty minutes. I hear it is pretty good," Eric suggested.

"I'll take a rain-check if that's okay. They were going to call me this afternoon," Bert said. She knew it was a lame excuse but it was the best she could come up with quickly. Jeff and she liked going to afternoon shows whenever he got enough time off. They always held hands and shared popcorn. Sometimes they would walk out of one show and into the one next door. She was not ready to hold hands in a show just yet.

They had a long leisurely lunch and he had her back at the house by three-thirty. She thanked him and set a time for the following evening.

Walking back in the house she felt the stillness closing in on her. She turned around at the door and saw Arthur Plant walking around the cul-de-sac. He was obviously watching her arrive and enter the house. She walked inside and quickly locked the dead bolt. Picking up her portable phone, she went out to Jeff's workshop. She would work on the corner cabinet Jeff had been making for Elizabeth and Max for Christmas. He had the carcass done and she got out several of his panel bits; putting the first one in his router. She had watched Jeff do it many times. She often helped him when he needed another set of hands. He often told her she should make something herself. He knew she had the talent. She had the doors done for the lower section and was starting on the stiles for the glass doors she was placing on the upper half of the cabinet when Elizabeth called. She looked up at the clock and it was eight thirty in the evening. She answered the phone and turned off her dust collection system so she could hear her daughter. She talked as she doused the lights and walked back into the house, automatically setting the security system.

While she was finishing her call from her daughter, she noticed the blinking light on her answering service telling her she had two calls. The first one was from Art asking her to dinner the next evening. It sent chills down her spine. There was no way she was going to be seen with that man. He sure has his nerve, she thought. He knew Nancy and she had been good friends and he must know Bertha knew what a stinker he had been to Nancy. The second call was from Eric. He wanted to know if she got in all right. Why wouldn't she, she smiled to herself. She called and they talked for a half-hour. She felt much calmer when she went to her bedroom and retired for the night.

Chapter Eight

Elizabeth was surprised her mother had made plans for dinner with friends on their last evening without talking to her about it, but Max seemed so pleased she didn't argue.

They arrived at Mary and Steve's at six o'clock. Eric met them at the door. He greeted Max with a hearty handshake. It was obvious to Elizabeth that Max had met these people before. Eric took Elizabeth's hand and thanked her for coming. They walked into the living room and Mary called out for them to join them in the kitchen. "Steve is trying to slice up some cheese," she laughed. "It looks like we will be eating chunk cheese."

Eric introduced his sister and brother-in-law to Elizabeth. They enjoyed an hour of conversation and then Eric said they had reservations at the club in ten minutes so they had better leave.

Eric drove again and they piled into Mary's car. They arrived at the club and were greeted by the hostess. "Back again Bert? And you brought more people this time," she smiled. "Hello Eric, good to see you again."

Bert smiled and said, "Yes, this is my daughter Elizabeth."

"I have a lovely window table for you," the hostess smiled.

They walked into a very crowded room. Bert was happy to see the club doing so well. They had worried about it's being able to support itself, the first few years of the restaurant's existence.

Enjoying a leisurely meal, they were home again by nine o'clock.

The first thing Elizabeth said as they entered the house, "how long have you known Eric, mother?"

"Not long," she smiled and went to her room. Elizabeth followed Bert into her walk-in closet.

"Mother that's no answer," her daughter stated, emphatically.

"Elizabeth! Let your mother get ready for bed. She owes you no explanation." Max said walking up behind his wife. "We had a good time with very interesting and entertaining people. You should be glad she has such good friends up here," Max told his wife.

"Well, I smell a rat. There is something you two are not telling me," Elizabeth said.

"You surprise me, Elizabeth. I thought you had a good time this evening. I think that is all that matters. Now, listen to your husband, dear and let me get dressed for bed," Bert smiled at her daughter.

Elizabeth knew that look her mother gave her and realized she would get no more information from her so she left the room. I'll get it out of Max; she smiled. He could never keep anything from her.

Elizabeth's husband followed her out of the room. If she thinks she can interrogate me, she has another think coming. He smiled at her retreating back. He knew he would be in for the third degree when they went to their own room. Elizabeth gave up too easily. He was right but he stuck to his guns and refused to tell her anything he knew Bertha thought was none of his wife's business.

The next morning every-one was all smiles; but Elizabeth looked very thoughtful and it bothered Bert. Maybe she should have told her more but she was not up to a third degree the night before her daughter was leaving. Elizabeth and Max left for their home shortly after breakfast but not until she made Bertha promise to spend Thanksgiving with them. She smiled as they left and went into the quiet, empty house. The only noise to be heard was the rattle of the dishes as she cleared the counter and cleaned up the remains of breakfast.

The phone rang several times but she left the answering service pick it up. She would screen all calls from now on. She did not want an argument with Art. She did not even want to talk to him.

Chapter Nine

She had not heard from Eric for several days, when Mary called and asked her to lunch. "I'd love it. I'm a little bored. I didn't even go to my workshop today. I don't seem to care if school keeps or not," Bert laughed.

"Then we can take a long lunch and do some shopping," Mary told her.

"Great! I need so many things. How much time can you spare?" Bert asked.

"I've got all day," Mary laughed.

"Would you like to go to Traverse? We can have lunch there; I'll drive," Bert told her.

.   "Sounds like fun. Why don't you come by about eleven and we can get to Traverse in time for lunch." Mary told her. She hung up the phone and went in to take her shower.

At Eleven o'clock she pulled up in front of Mary's home and she came running out the door, climbed into Bert's car and said, "To Traverse City James, and don't spare the horses."

They had a wonderful ride over to Traverse City. The sun was shinning, and the clouds were white and puffy. She loved a day like today. The traffic was so light they saw very few cars on the whole trip up Mancelona Road to 131 south.

Bert found out through Mary that Eric had been called back to California and would be calling her this weekend.

"I wondered what happened to him," Bert smiled.

"He left early in the morning. He had some kind of an emergency, and asked me to tell you he would be here for Thanksgiving. He wondered if you would like to join us."

"My daughter made me promise to spend it down state," Bertha told her. "I'm surprised he is coming here again so soon but I can imagine your excitement in having him for the Holiday."

The two women went shopping and Mary laughed at the long list of items Bertha needed.

"Well! I have everything on my shopping list. I guess we can go home now," Bertha laughed in return.

The women took a leisurely ride home and just outside of town, Bertha stopped at a little fruit stand. The two women bought enough fruits and vegetables to last them both two weeks and almost depleted the women's supplies. "I stop here whenever I am in town," Bert told Mary after they were back in the car and driving down the road. "She has the best produce around and always has a friendly smile when I pull up."

"If you buy this much every time, I don't blame her for smiling. She is going to have to restock before anyone else arrives. She does have the best produce I've seen in a long time," Mary agreed.

Bert dropped Mary off after the two made a pact to have lunch together every week.

Chapter Ten

Bertha called the moving company on Monday and several days later, she had all the treasures she had left in storage back in California stacked in piles in her entrée hall.

She worked all week trying to find places to put everything. She cut all the boxes up, piling them in a neat stack and tying them with string to put out for the rubbish collector to pick-up. She had put off going into the garage and it was now the time; she had to go in, and face the two Harleys parked there. Bert knew she needed to start them and let them run for a while, but she just could not get on Jeff's and ride it. Her bike was a low-rider and much easier for her to handle but that was not the real reason. With a deep sigh, she went out and looked at the bikes. She walked over and started hers and it kicked right in. Jeff's bike was a little harder and by the time she got it started, the noise was deafening, and smoke from the exhaust was thick as pea soup in the closed garage. Dummy, you should have opened the big door. Get your head out of the sand she reprimanded herself.

She pushed the automatic door opener and the sun came blazing through. Eric was on the other side of the door.

"I wondered what all the noise was about," he said in greeting. "Wow! Are they beautiful," he added, admiring the bikes. "They're Screaming Eagle 2000's aren't they? Who did the custom paint job? Look at that instrument panel. I've never seen so much chrome. Who cut yours down?" He never took his eyes off the cycles.

Bertha laughed, "Hello stranger, I'm glad to see you too," she smiled. "I'm pleased you like them. What brings you to these parts, so soon?" she asked.

"It's a long story and I wanted to tell you in person," Eric told her. "First tell me where these came from."

"California," she answered. "The low rider is mine and the other bike was Jeff's. I had them shipped with my other things. Jeff's is too big for me but he had mine chopped before he brought it home to me. His bike weighs about 350 pounds. Mine isn't much better but at least I can reach the ground and hold it up when I stop. I was going for a ride on my bike, would you like to join me," she said. She did not know why she asked him, but she had blurted it out and he seemed pleased.

"Would I ever! Do you have another helmet?"

She went over to the old trunk in the corner and pulled out her and Jeff's matching helmets. He quickly put it on and laughed. The laugh sounded just like Jeff's coming through the helmet. Bertha felt a strange feeling go through

57

her body. Why had she allowed another man to wear Jeff's things? She thought to herself. But, what was the matter with her; Jeff was gone; he would want someone else to enjoy his things. He was that kind of man. As though Eric read her mind, he gave her a weak smile and said, "Thank you, now how about lunch. I'm starved. I thought we might go to the club."

Snapping out of her doldrums she said, "Sounds good to me. That was where I was headed anyway." She had planned to meet Mary there in a half an hour.

They rode over to the club and parked in one of the parking places. There were not many spaces left. The restaurant was crowded for the middle of the week. They were shown to a table in the bar area but Bertha did not mind. There did not seem to be anyone smoking.

After they had ordered a drink Bert asked, "Well what is your big news?"

"I am really excited. I am going to open an office here in town and I'm only here for a week to look for a place."

"How soon do you think you will be ready for business?" Bert asked. "I'll be your first customer," Bert told him, trying to keep the excitement out of her voice. However, she could not keep the smile from her face. That was the trouble having dimples, the smile always showed.

"I want to be in and running by the first of the year, so that doesn't give me much time to find a building and a place to stay. I don't want to impose on Mary and Max for as long as it takes to build me a home here in Michaywe," he told her.

Just then, a voice said, "Hello brother. I've been waiting to hear how soon you wanted me to pick you up, I even took my cell-phone to the pool; but I see you found better transportation," she smiled at Bert.

"I rented a car at the airport. I got to thinking on the flight over; I should really have my own transportation. I have a million things to accomplish in very little time," he told his sister.

"May I sit down? Did you forget we had a lunch date?" she asked Bertha. "I took in a swim first so brother, don't comment on my hair," she rattled on.

"Please join us," Bert laughed. "I was just about to offer my lower level to Eric. It has two bedrooms, a small kitchen, living area and its own entrance. He can come and go as he pleases and in bad weather he can use the main entrance, if he doesn't want to plow a path to the back door."

"That sounds wonderful, Eric. I've seen her lower level and it is as big as most houses," Mary told him.

"I don't want to impose on you Bert. I wasn't hinting for a place to hang my hat," he told her.

"Don't kid yourself; there is a method to my madness. I will feel better having someone else in the house at night and I have a big job for a couple strong men," She told him.

"You name it. It's done," Eric smiled. "You have taken a load off my mind. Now all I need is a building, a lot and a builder for my new house."

"You better look at the job first. I need my exercise room moved from the lower level to my sunroom. I figure I will use it more if it is on the main floor," Bert said.

"I'll get Steve to come over after work tonight and he and Eric will get it done in no time," Mary laughed. "Eric you will stay with us until you get your things here and move into your new digs, won't you?"

"Sure sis, but I will be gone a lot. I thought maybe you ladies might help me find a building downtown," He said.

"I'd love to," Mary said. "Do you have the time?" she asked Bert.

"I have nothing but time. I finally have everything put away and I have been trying to find something else to do," Bert answered her. "I know of a couple of lots too, you might want to look at."

"Let's order. I'm anxious to get started," Eric said.

They ordered, and talked, and talked, and talked. "We better get out of here before they throw us out. You were the guy that wanted to get going so fast," Bert laughed.

The three left the restaurant and headed for Bert's home.

Chapter Eleven

Bertha and Eric returned the bikes to the garage and piled into Mary's waiting car.

They rode into town and Bertha introduced Eric to Mr. Smith, her friend and Real Estate broker. Smith knew of a vacant building on the edge of the downtown's main road, and offered to take them there. They got into Smith's car and rode out just past the golf course. It was perfect and Eric put an offer in on it immediately. They drove back to the office and Mr. Smith called to tell his client of the offer. It was too good to refuse so Eric now had a building.

"Now, we would like to know what you have in lots in Michaywe. Something he can put a ranch style home on," Bert told Smith. He said he had nothing available that would be large enough for the size ranch Eric wanted to build, but he would start checking around.

The three left and returned to Michaywe. "I think I know of a lot that might be available. The one around the corner from you Mary," Bert told them on the way to her home.

"You know, I'll bet you're right. He had it on the market quite a while ago, but wanted too much money for it. He now has own sign up. I'll bet cash will bring the price down. His home phone number is on the sign. Let's call him," Mary said excitedly. "That is if you don't mind being so close to my place. It's almost half way between Bert's home and ours."

They pulled up to the lot and Eric jumped out and assisted his sister and Bert from the car. They walked the entire lot and Eric said, "This is too good to be true. Get the man's number off the sign sis and we will go to Bert's and call him."

They hurried to the house and as Bertha fixed coffee, Mary set out the coffee cups and fixings.

"Would you call him, Schlick? You know how to deal with people up here. Try to get a good deal but get me that lot," Eric smiled.

Bert went to the phone and called the number that she took off the sign. An older gentleman answered. She introduced herself and explained she had a friend who was looking for a lot and as a neighbor, she thought of his. He wanted about four thousand dollars too much for it and Bert told him so. "You won't have to pay a commission and we will handle the closing." She waited for him to digest what she had said and they talked about other things for a few minutes. The gentleman finally agreed to Bert's price and she said she would send him a contract in the over night mail.

They celebrated that evening at the clubhouse. "This is becoming a habit," the hostess smiled at Eric.

"It will soon be more than a habit. I'm opening a branch office in town and I'm going to build a home here in Michaywe. I plan on having a lot of meals here," he told her.

"Have you found a builder yet?" the hostess asked.

"I am going to see Mrs. Schlinkenmayer's builder tomorrow. I understand he did all the renovations on this building," Eric told her.

"You can't get better. He did this and the golf course clubhouse. I have never heard anything bad about him and Mrs. Schlinkenmayer is always singing his praises," she smiled, handed them their menu and said, "Enjoy! I hear the chef's special is terrific." She walked back to the front desk.

"You sure have a way with her. She did more talking to you than I've heard her talk to anyone else," Mary laughed.

They took her advice and got the special. They were not unhappy. It was delicious but they did not think they would have room for dessert.

Eric insisted on paying the bill. The three left and walked out to Mary's car. "Did you want to go see the builder with us tomorrow?" Eric asked.

"I'm sorry but I have to be home tomorrow for a delivery. Why don't you and Bert go? She knows him personally and can introduce you to him," Mary suggested.

"Do you have time, Schlick?" Eric asked.

"Yes, of course, but why don't I call him and see when he will be in," Bert smiled and dialed the builders number on her cell phone. His sister

Jan answered. She was in charge of the office and Bert enjoyed lunch with her whenever Jan could take the time. "I have a gentleman here Jan, that wants an appointment with your brother. We were wondering if he has the time tomorrow," Bert said.

"He will be back at four o'clock tomorrow, if that is convenient," Jan said. "He can give you an hour before his next appointment."

Bert relayed the message to Eric. He nodded his approval and Bert finalized the appointment. "How about lunch Friday?" Jan asked.

"I'll let you know when we come in; if that's soon enough," Bert told her.

"Sure! I'll be glad to see you again. How is everything?" Jan asked. Jan had heard Bert was back in town but had not wanted to bother her until she was sure she wanted company.

"Under the circumstances, it couldn't be better, friend. I'm looking forward in seeing you too. I've got heaps to tell you. I'll let you go; I know you're busy. My news can wait," Bert told her. She knew Jan would be thrilled she was moving back home. Since Jan had her home built in Michaywe' they would be able to see more of each other.

Mary pulled up in front of Bert's home, dropped off her passengers and drove off. Eric and Bertha waved at her as she pulled out of the circular drive.

The next day Eric arrived early and said, "We have a couple hours to kill and I need some things from town. Do you want to ride along?

Maybe you have some shopping to do too."

Bert laughed, "I think your sister and I bought enough while we were in Traverse City to last me a while, but I'll be glad to ride along. I was only going to write e-mails to friends in California this afternoon but I have all evening to do that. I would like to go in for a few minutes and change into some walking shoes. I know the builder will want to walk the lot as soon as possible.

"I'd like to be there when he marks it. I know where I would like the house to set, if it is feasible," Eric said.

"We could go and mark it ourselves if you want," Bertha told him.

"Do you know how to do that?" Eric asked.

"You forget, Jeff was in Real Estate here for several years, before his company moved us to California and I was his assistant," she smiled. "I wish I had a nickel for every lot I tramped around on with him."

"Let's do it now. Can we get it done in time for our meeting?" He asked.

"If we get lucky. Let me get my long tape and Geiger counter. We can at least get the house more or less placed where you'd like it. The builder will want to do the final placing," Bert told him and went to the garage while Eric made several calls on his cell phone. She got her tools, found some stakes, tape, and the Geiger counter. She walked back into the house and said, "I could use some help. We need the stakes, sledgehammer and ribbon; I left in the garage. I'll get my plat maps." Jeff had plat maps of the entire complex and she often wondered whenever she ran across them, why she kept them around.

Eric laughed and went into the garage, lifted the door and placed everything in his trunk and they headed for his new lot.

As luck would have it, they found the first surveyor's stake almost immediately. It was not difficult following Jeff's plat maps to find the remaining three stakes.

In a little over an hour they had staked and taped the entire lot. Standing on the road and looking at their handy work, the bright yellow tape traced the corners of the plat.

"This lot is large enough to put almost any size ranch you want to build on it," Bert told him.

"Yes, I am really looking forward to our meeting with the builder. We better get going. I don't want to keep him waiting," Eric said.

Holding the door for Bert, she smiled and got into the passenger seat.

Chapter Twelve

Jan met them at the door and gave Bert a big hug. "I've missed you so much. I hope you are here for a long visit this time," she said.

"I'm back for good. I've moved back into my home in Michaywe. We will have lots of time to talk about it but first I want you to meet Eric. He is looking for a builder and I suggested Jeff might do a good job," Bert laughed.

"Welcome Eric; don't pay any attention to her. She is one of my brother's biggest fans. I can't tell you how many people she has steered our way," Jan smiled up at him.

Jeff walked out of his office. "Did I hear right. You're back for good?" He said to Bert. "Look out Jan, with her around we are going to be turning away clients."

"As if you would ever turn away a client," Bert laughed. She introduced Eric to Jeff and the two men shook hands.

Eric admired the ease Schlick had with everyone. There must be something terribly wrong with Art for her to be so short with him.

"Come into my office and let me make some notes on what your needs are and how large a home you want to build," Jeff suggested.

"Sounds good. Bert, will you sit in and give any ideas you might have?" He asked. "This will be the first home I have had built from scratch and I have a dozen ideas, but they may not be practical," Eric said guiding her into Jeff's office. They took seats across from Jeff's desk and started talking. They were just finishing when Jeff's next appointment appeared at the door.

"I'll get some plans drawn up and get back to you the first of the week if that is soon enough," Jeff said. "It will give me enough time to check out the lot. I'm sure by looking at the plat maps, it will be adequate but I'd like to check and see what it looks like now that Bert has plotted it out."

Bert knew he would do any final checking but at least it was a starting point and Jeff and his men would not have to look for the iron lot markers.

"I'll be back in California next week but I am coming east with some of my things the following month, so I won't be around for a couple weeks. Let me give you my cell phone and fax number. If there is anything you need, you can call me and then fax any papers necessary," Eric told him. The two men shook hands and Bert and Eric left the office.

Walking outside Eric said, "Guess I better change my name."

"Why would you want to do that?" Bert asked.

"It looks like you have a thing for men named Jeff," he smiled.

"Don't change it. I like the name Eric," she told him. "What is this about your leaving this weekend?" Bert inquired.

"Yes! I may as well start moving my stuff here, now that I have a place to live," he smiled at her. "We'll be over this evening and start moving your exercise equipment upstairs. I was sorry Steve could not do it last night but he should be home about six. I promised Mary I would be home for dinner. I wanted to have dinner out with you but she is planning something. I have no idea what she is up to. How about dinner tomorrow evening," he said as he pulled into her drive.

"I'm sorry; I promised the group I used to sing with to come to their gig. They are trying to get me to return," she told him. "I think I might join again; they are a lot of fun. They are singing for the senior home in town and then they always go out afterward. I won't be able to sing this time but I told them I'd tag along."

"Well, let's make it the following evening then. I'm leaving the next day," Eric told her.

"I'll check my calendar," Bert laughed. "Silly!" she said as she looked at his shocked face. "Of course, we'll have dinner on Friday night."

He picked her up that Friday and they went to a quiet little restaurant in town.

He noticed immediately she was not herself. He took her hand and said, "Your friends death is really bothering you, isn't it?" He knew she had spent the evening before with the group of singers and that must have been the topic of their conversation.

"Yes, I'm sorry. I tried not to let it show, but talking to the girls brought it all back. They told me he was running with another friend of ours and we are all worried about her," Bert told him.

"Do you think he is dangerous?" Eric asked.

"I'd bet on it. All I know is; she would never cut her own throat. She had a nervous fit one afternoon on the golf course when she had a bloody nose. I have to do something. He can't get away with it," Bert told Eric.

"I'll make a deal with you. If you will wait until I get back and set tight until then. I'll make your case the first one on my docket at our new office. We will get together and solve her death one way or the other," He told her.

"I don't want to have you get into any trouble your first week here," Bertha told him.

"Don't worry about me. I have more contacts here than you think I do. I'll get on it as soon I get back and settled. Do I have your word; you'll stay away from him until I return?" He squeezed her hand.

"I would be foolish not to agree. You will be able to do more in a day then I could do in a month. Thank you, Eric. I'll sleep easier tonight," Bert smiled and removed her hand and started on her salad.

"Now let's forget it and enjoy our evening. We can't do anything about it right now and this salad looks too good to let set and wilt," He smiled at her.

Chapter Thirteen

Eric left the morning after their dinner. It had been a quiet few hours and both tried to make light of the evening. He called before leaving and she rolled over in bed and tried to go back to sleep after his call.

She got up early and attempted to keep busy. She washed windows, mopped floors and did every little chore she could think of. Evening finally arrived and she retired before ten. She tried to read but the words did not make any sense to her, so she watched a little television; that was worse. Around two o'clock she finally fell into a fitful sleep.

She got up the next morning at six and got ready for church. She was thrilled to see so many of her old friends had not left for Florida yet. She stayed for social hour and then went to lunch with a gang of them. Following her usual Sunday pattern afterward she drove herself to town to do some shopping. She really did not need very much but it kept her mind busy. Later she went to a movie, then home and to bed.

Rising at six again Monday, she again got busy and started cleaning house. Smiling, she thought, great pal now what are you going to do.

You've already cleaned this place once and it sure doesn't need it again. As if she had read her mind, Jan called to ask her to lunch. "How about Chinese, for a change." she suggested.

Looking up at the clock, Bert noticed it was eleven thirty and she had not taken time for breakfast. "Good choice. I'll pick you up in about forty minutes, okay?" she asked.

"I'm looking forward to it. I'll tell the secretary I am taking an extra long lunch hour. We have so much, catching up to do," Jan laughed.

She pulled up in front of Jan's building at the exact time agreed upon, and Jan was waiting at the door. "I see you're still a bug about being on time," she smiled.

"Old habits die hard. Sometimes I don't even have to stay on schedule but I do. Do you know; I still clean house on Monday and wash on Tuesday. Isn't that silly? I found myself re-cleaning places that didn't need it the first time," Bert laughed.

"Lady, you need something to do," Jan returned her laughter. "Maybe when Eric returns he will have something better in mind," Jan smiled waiting for Bert to say something.

Bert did; she changed the subject. She drove them to the restaurant located near the large discount store she shopped in, and was able to find a parking place right in front of the restaurant.

Exiting the car they met two of Jan's friends, leaving the same establishment they were about to enter. Stopping to talk for a few minutes gave Bert time to decide how much she was willing to divulge to Jan about Eric. She decided she might as well tell her everything. She would pull it out of her anyway.

They were shown a booth and Jan said, "I'm starved. I didn't have time for breakfast today. I'm going to go to the buffet and start filling a plate."

"Sounds good, I didn't take time for breakfast either," Bert told her.

They came back to the table and before Bertha got the first fork full up to her mouth Jan said, "Okay friend, lets hear about that hunk you brought to the office. Where did you find him and how serious is it."

Bert smiled. She might as well start explaining. She would not be able to eat until she did. "He is a friend I met on the trip here from California. We met at a campsite and he was very helpful. We are just friends," Bert said. "Now let me eat something."

"Okay but hurry up. You're not going to stop there", Jan laughed.

Bert ate a little but knew Jan was getting impatient with her so she told her about the scooter and then about Branson. Pausing to eat again, Jan asked. "What is this name "Schlick", he calls you every so often?"

Bert explained it to her and she said, "It sounds to me like you are a little more than just friends."

"Don't start. He is going to stay in my lower level while your brother builds his home, and I don't want any rumors going around about the two of us," Bert said.

Jan laughed. "In your lower lever! Pretty nice; very convenient," she teased.

"You're too much. If you don't stop I'll talk him out of using your brother," Bert laughed.

"You wouldn't do that. You want him to have the best," Jan laughed.

"Boy are we getting big headed," Bert teased her back.

"That's your fault. You keep telling my brother how good he is and it's gone to his head," Jan laughed.

They enjoyed the lunch and before they left she had filled Jan in on all the events in Bertha's life for the past year and a half, along with her true feelings about Eric.

"I think you are crazy to worry about the age difference. You never did act your age," Jan was teasing her again.

"We'll see. He may not be that certain about his feelings either. Six months in the same vicinity should prove something," Bert smiled. "Come on, I have to get you back to work," she told her.

"I think Jeff has some preliminary plans drawn up, if you want to take a peek," Jan told her, as they were parking in front of her office.

"I'd love to," Bert answered and followed her inside the building.

Jan went into the architects' office and brought out a bundle of plans. "See what you think," she said

.   Bert looked over the plans and commented, "I know he wants a walk out basement."

"Yes! There will be one; but he hasn't drawn that up yet. He will have it done by the end of the week," Jan told her.

"Well I for one love the plans he has completed. I'll let Eric know how hard you're working on it," Bert told her.

"He calls you that often?" Jan asked, lifting her eyebrows.

"Yes!" Bert said and added, "I'm going to go before you start pumping me again." Bert laughed, gave her a big hug and left the building.

She drove home in silence. She had really cleared her head while talking to Jan. Jan had been a big help in Bert seeing things more clearly. She knew she would have to keep busy or her mind would not stop pumping. She did not even go into the house when she got home. She went into the workshop and put on her coveralls. She was still working four hours later when she heard her neighbor from around the corner tap on her side window. She looked up and saw Annette peeking in. She went out to the garage door; opened it and greeted her friend.

"Hi, stranger. I thought I'd come and invite you to dinner." Annette said. "I'm alone tonight and I'll be darned if I am going to cook. Why don't you break away and come to the clubhouse with me. You should take a rest. I took my walk earlier and saw you out here. You've been here most of the day. What in the world are you working on?"

"A new corner cabinet for Elizabeth's new house. I have most of it cut and assembled and was getting ready to start the final assembly. Give me about five minutes," Bert told her. "I have to get clamps on this before the glue sets." Bert and Annette went back into the workshop and Bert picked up two one-hand clamps. She put them on the two boards she had biscuit-joined together and set the clamps. "Jeff would have had this thing completed by now, but at least it keeps me busy."

"Are those going to hold it?" Annette asked looking at the little clamps.

"No; I put these on until I can get my large pipe clamps secured and tightened. There, now I can go get some lipstick on and we can go," Bert said, as she finished gluing and clamping the three boards.

"Don't you want to change first?" Annette asked.

"That might be best," Bert said and unzipped her jumpsuit, smiling at her friend. "Now do I look good enough to go?" she laughed.

"Good enough, if that's as good as it gets," Annette teased her.

The two women got into Bert's car and headed for the club.

There was a good size group there for a weeknight, and they had to wait for ten minutes to get a table in the dining room. "I'm sorry for the wait," the hostess said and showed them to their table.

"If we had brought your handsome friend, we probably wouldn't have had to wait," Annette laughed.

"You might be right," Bert laughed. "While we are on the subject of Eric; I have rented him my lower level until his house is built. So you will see his car there quite a bit. He is starting an office in town and is moving here as soon as he gets things arranged at his California office."

"I wondered," Annette smiled. "I'll bet a dozen people have been speculating. You have been seen with him quite a bit lately. If you don't want to talk about it, that's all right. It is no one's business but your own."

"That's all right. I figured some tongues would start wagging. You've probably had a tough time. Everyone knows we're friends," Bert smiled. "After all, Jeff has only been gone a little over two years, but if anyone asks; tell them I met him a couple months ago and leave it at that. Eric and I have become friends. His sister and brother-in-law live in Michaywe and we were bound to run into one another."

"Don't get me wrong. I think it is great; you have someone to take you out once in a while. It must get pretty lonely for you. You and Jeff seemed so happy and inseparable."

"We were; it was a terrible shock when he died. You know he was never ill. There was just no warning," Bert explained. "I want to thank you for the lovely contribution the gang made to the Heart Fund. I sent thank you notes but I want to tell everyone personally. We had so many friends and colleagues show up at the memorial service; he was so well thought of. I had him cremated and his ashes strewn around our favorite campsite. He loved the outdoors so, and said if anything happened to him, he wanted his ashes to be scattered among the trees. I sold our big rig and bought that smaller one I drove here from California."

"We all miss him. He was one of a kind," Annette said.

"They don't make many like him," Bert smiled. "He could not have been a better help-mate. We discussed many times, what we would do if one or the other died. He always said I should find someone else, I was too good a wife to be left alone," this time Bert had to force a smile through the tears she felt forming.

Annette smiled and said, "What are you going to have tonight?" trying to change the subject. Her friend should have a nice night out instead of remembering the past. She really was happy Bert might have found a new male friend. She should have a party for him when he finally moved here, and made a mental note to pass it by the gang.

They ate until there was no room for dessert and laughingly told the waitress to bring the wheelbarrow to help get them out to the car.

The two women went outside into the warm fall evening. "This is probably my favorite time of the year," Annette commented.

"Mine too. Too bad it is followed by snow," Bert laughed. "Is the gang going up to the U.P. again this year?"

"Of course! They wouldn't miss it. Will you be going?" Annette asked her.

"I doubt it. No one has said anything to me. I think they feel funny having an odd number going," Bert said.

"Nonsense, that's only in your head. Think about it. Maybe Eric would like to go," Annette smiled.

"You're as bad as Jan. She is pushing it too," Bertha laughed. "Come on, I'm going to get you home before you have us going north together."

"You're such a moralist," Annette laughed.

The women climbed into Bert's car and she drove Annette home. Arriving at her place, they made a date for later in the week to do some shopping.

Bert drove into her garage. She was more tired then she realized. She went into the house and did not stop to check on the glue job she had left. She knew she would have a scraping job tomorrow but she did not care. She should have gone in and removed the excess before it got too hard. She striped, put on her P.J.'s and curled up in bed with a book.

The phone rang, giving her a start. It was ten-thirty at night. She stiffened herself for bad news. Softly saying hello into the phone, she heard Eric's voice. "I hope I didn't disturb you."

"No, I was just reading. She noted it was only seven-thirty in California. He probably did not think of the time difference.

"Oh Golly, I just looked at the clock. It's late there, isn't it? I am sorry," He said.

"Don't worry about it. It isn't that late. How are things going there?" Bert asked.

"Not as well as I'd hoped. The fellow I wanted to manage this office didn't work out and now I have to start interviewing again," Eric said.

"What about the woman that has been your right arm for the last four years," Bert suggested.

"I don't know. She is more than qualified, but she is a woman, and I don't know if the rest of the staff will accept her," He told her.

"Then, I'd get a new staff," Bert answered. "You did nothing but rave about her and your secretary, at dinner the last night you were here. In my opinion, for what it is worth; you should at least give her a chance at the job."

"You're right of course. I have been wrestling with the idea all week. I'll talk to her tomorrow," he laughed. "Thank you. Why is it when I talk to you, everything falls into place?"

"You already made the decision. You only needed someone to confirm it," Bert told him "How did your secretary take the news? Is she willing to move here?" She asked.

"She was delighted but, this means I'll be here until the first of the year. Will my apartment be available?" He asked.

"Oh, I suppose so. If no other good looking young men knock at my door," She laughed. "Will you be here for any of the Holidays?"

"Definitely for Christmas but I don't know about Thanksgiving yet. I really wanted to see my sister and check on the office. I was wondering if I could impose on you to help me get it decorated and furnished." He said, and then not waiting for an answer, "I'm sending my secretary and her husband out to set up the office, next month. Do you think you could show them around and maybe find them a place to live? I don't want to impose on our friendship but you know the area so well.   If you are going to be too busy please say so."

"Don't give it another thought. Yes, on both the office and the secretary. I was getting very bored and your doing me a favor, but are you sure I'm the right person to decorate your office?" She questioned.

"You've got to be kidding! I've seen your place and wouldn't change a thing. Your taste is impeccable." He answered.

"That's the first time I've heard it called that, but thank you, kind sir," She said. "Let me know when they are coming and I'll pick them up at the Traverse City airport."

"You're the best. I won't worry about them as long as you are taking care of them." They may want a house, so you might want to alert Fred."

"I'll call him first thing tomorrow," Bertha laughed.

"It might take some time for them to get acquainted enough with the area to know where they want to live. I think they would be perfect in one of those new areas our builder is just finishing up."

"I'll check on that also," she began to smile.

"If they are a little short on a down payment, let me know. Their money may be tied up. If they find something right away, I don't want them to miss out on a house if they find one. I'll foot the bill until they can pay me back. I want to keep them happy."

"Will do boss; let me take care of it," Bert's smile became a laugh.

They talked for several more minutes and then they said good night and hung up the phones. Bertha rolled over and fell asleep almost immediately.

Chapter Fourteen

Bertha was finishing the corner cabinet when she got the phone call she had been expecting for a week. "Hi Schlick! Are you ready for company? Hazel and Carl are leaving here the end of next week. They will be flying into the Traverse City Airport about three forty your time."

"Great! I just finished my project. They are coming at a perfect time. I need something to look forward to. I talked to Fred and he said he faxed you the papers and the building now belongs to you; taxes and all," Bert laughed. "The furnace man put in a new filter and cleaned all the points so it is ready to go. When the inspector I hired checked it all out, he said he could not find anything wrong with it and the county inspector has approved it for occupancy."

"How did the roof look? He mentioned it only slightly in his report," Eric asked her.

"It looked good. I was up there with him. I don't like a poured roof but it looks like you have a few years left before you have to decide what you want to do with it," Bert told him.

"You went up on that roof. You crazy nut," He laughed. "You sound like you have some ideas on what to do with the roof?"

"I'd wait until winter is over and lift the roof for more space. Then you can put some trusses up and have room for a couple private offices up there," She told him.

"That sounds good. Do you think Carl would have time yet this year to do it? It would keep him busy," Eric asked.

"Probably if I can get a team together and the snow doesn't come early. Things are slowing down here right now, but because hunting season will be coming in two weeks everything stops around here." She told him. "The schools close and a lot of the businesses shut their doors for the first day of deer season. It is almost impossible yet this year but I'll sure try. Even our builder takes a week off and goes to his cabin. He says he goes hunting but I think it is just an excuse for him and his buddies to play cards, have a couple beers, and tell each other jokes. I'll see what I can do. If I can get it roughed in, then Carl can finish it."

"Well! When he arrives you can talk to him," Eric said.

"Don't worry about him not having enough to do. He will be busy painting, moving walls, and placing the furniture I've purchased," She laughed. "This has been fun, spending someone else's money."

"I've seen the bills. I'm surprised you could do it so inexpensively; but then that's why I call you Schlick," he laughed. "Well, I better let you get back to bed. You're going to be busy this next week. Call if you need anything. Good night

Schlick; miss you," He said and hung up.

Bertha went to sleep, thinking of all the things she wanted to complete before Carl and Hazel arrived.

Chapter Fifteen

Bert got the roof in the process of being raised the very next day. As usual, her friend Jeff came to her rescue. He had a team of roofers over to the building before seven o'clock and they had the roof almost off before she arrived at noon. She was lucky he had the men available and he said it would only take a few days to rough it all in and put it under a new roof. She would have to pray for clear skies. She went to Jeff's office and he had his draftsman design the roof and told them how many trusses would be needed. While she was there, he called and ordered them and told the dealer they had to be there by the first of the week. They faxed Eric and he thanked Jeff and told him there would be a check there before the trusses arrived. He would send the check on over-night service.

Jeff smiled as she left the room. "He is going to have to slow down when he moves here. I can't believe he wanted to get the check here immediately. I could have paid for them and he could pay me later."

She shrugged her shoulders. "That's his way." Bertha told him.

"He has sent me almost enough to pay off the new house. I told him I could wait but he sent it anyway," he smiled and walked Bert to her car.

The trusses were up and they were roofing it the day she drove to the airport to pick up Eric's secretary, Hazel Sanderson and her husband Carl.

Hazel and Carl recognized her as soon as they stepped through the gate. "How did you know it was me?" Bert asked.

"Eric gave us a pretty good description, right down to what you would probably be wearing," Hazel laughed.

"Was he right?" Bert asked.

"Yes, except for the chunky heeled, high fashion shoes. He didn't mention you were a fashion plate," Carl smiled.

"Let's get your luggage and get out of here. I'm dying to show you around," Bertha told the couple.

"We would love to find us a place to stay until we can look for a house," Carl said. "We both dislike motel rooms and would like to get into a house as soon as possible."

"You will stay with me, if that's alright. I have an apartment in the lower level that Eric will be using while his house is being built but he won't need it until January. By that time, we should have you in your own place. I thought I'd show you the office first. Tomorrow you can go to the bank and get your qualification papers started; then I'll take you to all the areas that have that priced home. I think you will be surprised how much home you can get for your money up here," Bertha told them.

"You sure have everything organized," Carl said, "but are you sure you want company. It may take a while for us to get into our own place."

"I'll be disappointed if you don't stay with me. I'll give you both a key to the house and you can come and go as you please. Eric said the first thing he wants us to do is get you a S.U.V. before our winter season really starts. He said to charge it to the company," Mary said.

"It looks like you two have thought of everything. He said we would be in good hands," Carl smiled.

Their first stop was the car dealership. It took them over an hour to pick out the car they wanted. Eric had called ahead and faxed any pertinent information the dealer might need to process the sale quickly. Bertha finely convinced them the Explorer was not too expensive and the company had already approved it.

"Can I get a matching one?" Carl asked the salesman. "I figure I will need separate transportation and we may as well get it now."

"I can have both cars here and ready by next week. One has to come from a dealer in Lansing and the other from Dearborn," the salesman said as he looked at his computer screen. "I'll need to get the pin-stripes you ordered put on them on Wednesday. That is the only day the man that does our detailing stops here," he added.

"Will that be all right?" Hazel asked Bertha. "Maybe we should rent a car until our new ones arrive."

"I don't think you'll have to," Bertha said. "I am sure the dealer will be happy to give you a loaner."

The salesman looked at her and smiled, "Of course. If you can come back this afternoon, I'll have one ready for you," he smiled.

When they left Carl started laughing. "He wasn't going to give us a loaner unless you pushed him into it," he said. "I'm glad you were with us. I probably would have paid for a rental."

"He is going to make enough on the two sales; that was the least he could do. They still make money even if we use the X plan." Eric's company was able to get fleet prices because they do work for the Car Companies. Eric's employees are able to purchase their cars at a discount and use his X plan. He will want at least another S.U.V. when he settles here and the salesman probably figured he had another sale coming soon."

"Would you like to go and see the office now? Then I will take you home and you can get settled. We won't cook tonight if that is okay with you. I thought we could go and have a nice meal at the clubhouse your first night here."

"That sounds nice but I'm afraid I will have to do some ironing before we go to dinner. I am sure after the search of my luggage; my clothes will need some work." Hazel told her.

"This is not a fancy club. They don't care what you wear as long as it is clothes. They are just happy you show up and enjoy their food. I've never seen them turn anyone away unless they were still in swim wear," Bert smiled at her.

"Do they have a pool?" Hazel asked excitedly.

"Two, one indoor and one outdoor. You will have time for a swim before dinner if you want," Bertha told her.

"No, but I would like one in the morning if that would not interfere with our schedule," she answered her.

"Schedules are to be flexible," Bert laughed and the couple began to relax.

Bert drove up to the building that would be Hazel's office and stopped the car. "Carl, there is an awful lot of work has to be done to the interior. It may be too much for one man. I can help, if you like. I know how to heft a hammer," Bert told him, as they exited the car and went toward the building. She got out her key and opened the door, handing another key to Carl. The smell inside the building was still musty, as it had not been opened for several days. "You will have to excuse the smell. I had the windows open for several hours while I measured for window treatments but I'm afraid it will take more than a few hours to get the stale smell out of here. The new wood on the roof helps a little. It smells much better upstairs."

"A little paint and new carpet should also help," Carl said. "Once I get the smell of new wood in here from the walls; it will make a big difference." He was looking at the prints Bert had left on the bench in the area that was to be the reception room.

"That's if you like the smell of wood," Ester teased. "How long before you can get my office built, dear?" she asked.

"Not too long. I'll get started on it as soon as I get this place painted," he said.

"I knew you were going to be swamped getting the walls up and finished so I have painters coming in on Monday and they said they should be out of here by the end of the week. They are going to paint all the walls and refinish the woodwork to a maple hue. They plan to stay until it is done, so there isn't much we can do before the first of the week. I thought you might want to go up north for a few days and I can show you our fall colors. We have lovely colors in Michaywe but you should see our famous Mackinaw Island. Eric thought it would be a good idea to get you a little acclimated, before I work you to death," Bert smiled.

"I read about Mackinaw Island. When we decided to move here, we studied up on your state. It was one of the reasons we thought we would like to live here. That and the snow. Carl has never seen snow," Hazel told her.

"He will see all of it he wants to see," Bertha laughed. "We expect a pretty tough winter this year. Don't ask me how they predict it but they seem to know what they are talking about. They can't predict the daily weather, but the seasons they are pretty good at," Bert smiled. "Well let's take the plans and go home. You can figure what you need and we will have them deliver it next week," she told Carl.

She drove them to her home and gave them both a key she had left for them on the kitchen counter before she went to pick them up. "I thought you would be more comfortable in the lower level. You will have more privacy that way and can come and go as you please," Bert said, showing them down the oak stairway. "As you can see, there is a back door, or you can use the front door."

Hazel was looking around the apartment and spotted the bathroom. "I'm dying for a nice hot shower. I feel like I haven't bathed in days," She said.

"You'll find towels in here," Bert said, showing her the linen closet in the hall. "If there is anything you need, let me know. There is shampoo and conditioner in the little basket on the back of the toilet. I'll let you two alone now, so you can get settled."

"You can take the first shower, honey. I'll take mine later," he told Hazel. "May I come up for a talk?" he asked Bert.

"Please!" Bertha said. "I'll fix a pot of coffee. Or if you would like something a little stronger there is some wine left from my late husband. I don't know much about wines but it is probably still okay."

"Thank you," he said and followed her up, fixed himself a glass of wine and joined her in the living room. He was pleased when he opened the bottle. It was red wine and did not need to be chilled.

Bert walked over to the fireplace and turned it on, taking some of the dampness out of the room. For some reason when the autumn leaves arrived, she always thought she needed a fire in the fireplace. "What do you have on your mind, Carl? Are you worried about moving here?"

"Far from it. I only wanted to thank you for making it so easy for us. This was mostly my idea. Hazel is as old fashioned as her name. You live and die where you are born. This is the first time I have been able to get her past Arizona and then that was only for a three day vacation," he told her.

"I had no idea. I thought you would be the one we would have to convince," Bert smiled at the young man.

He smiled in return and added, "I think you did more today in convincing her we were meant to move here than all the talking I've done. I like the idea of going away this weekend, if you're free. I'm sure she will get a kick out of seeing places we have only read about."

"I hope you won't be disappointed. It is a little touristy, but I have friends on the Island and we can see some of the inner Island that is out of the tourist path. I thought we could rent some bikes and ride the trail. It circles the entire Island," Bertha added.

They talked about the plans for the new office and Carl said he would get right on them that evening. "I am still on California time and probably will be awake for quite a while after you're asleep. I hope I won't disturb you if I work into the night."

"I wouldn't be able to hear you down there, but I don't think you will have a tough time adjusting to our clock. It was always more difficult for me to adjust when I returned to California than when I came to Michigan. One last thing, are you planning on going back for Christmas?" Bert asked.

"I honestly don't know. We discussed going back for a week at Thanksgiving, but her parents talked about coming here for Christmas," he told her.

"I just wondered. If you decide to go, you best make reservations now. They may already be filled up," she advised him.

"I don't think her parents should come during the winter months and I wish they would wait until we have a place for them to stay. Maybe we will go back for Christmas. I'll discuss it with Hazel. Will we have time tomorrow to start looking around?" He asked.

"Sure! We'll do that first. We can get up early and get right on it. Do you know what you want?" she asked.

"We will as soon as we go to the bank and talk to a loan officer," he laughed. "I'm hoping we can find something in the country or at least in a place like Michaywe," he said.

"We have enough variety here, you should be able to find what you're looking for," Bert told him.

"Well! I guess I better go shower. You probably want to freshen up a bit. When would you like us to come up?" he asked.

"Anytime you're ready. We can have a few snacks before we go and discuss our day tomorrow, and Carl, you and Hazel never need an invitation to come up stairs," she smiled at him and he smiled back leaving for his shower.

Bert had just gotten dressed when she heard them come up the stairs.

"Help yourself to anything you want," she yelled. "I'll be out in a couple minutes." She had put out snacks before she went to her room.

When she walked into the kitchen, she saw they had both taken a plate and several shrimp. Hazel had a diet coke and she noticed Carl had switched to cola.

"Try that cheese ball. It is one of my specialties," Bert said. "You can't find one with less fat in it. My late husband Jeff wouldn't tolerate fat of any kind, so I learned to make him one with very little in it. I'll bet you wouldn't have known it has almost no fat, if I hadn't told you."

Hazel took a cracker and tried the cheese ball. "You're right, this is delicious. Honey, you have to try this," she said to Carl. "I want this recipe."

Bert laughed and went to her kitchen desk drawer and pulled out a four by six card with the recipe on it. "I print these up by the dozen. Everyone thinks it's a big deal until they read how easy it is to make," she laughed.

Hazel read the card and laughed. "I can't believe this is all there is to it," she said. "Two low fat cream cheeses. One nonfat cream cheese, a medium container of blue cheese, and one stick of low-fat oleo. Mix and roll in crushed walnuts, if desired. This is great; I had prepared myself to a half-hour of weighing, measuring, chopping and mixing. It's good with or without the walnuts," she said, having another cracker lathered with a spoon of cheese ball.

"What are you too laughing at?" Carl asked walking into the kitchen. He had left them to watch the news on the television.

"I was getting a recipe from Bert," she smiled at him. When he left again, she said to Bert, "there is no way I'm going to let him know how easy this cheese ball is to make," and the women enjoyed another laugh.

They left for the club and when they arrived, the same hostess that had been enamored with Eric greeted them.

"Where is your handsome friend?" she asked.

"He had to leave but he'll be back later next month," Bert smiled.

Hazel smiled as they were seated at their table.

"You're right. I think she has a thing for our boss," Hazel commented. "It's funny how you work with someone for years and never think some women think he is handsome. I guess I'll have to pay closer attention."

"No honey! You keep your blinders on," Her husband laughed.

During dinner, Bert asked if they would like to rest a day and then she would take them to the Upper Peninsula.

Carl mentioned they did not know how much of their day the bank's loan officer would take.

"Well, you two, if we get a late start, we can plan to stay at a Bed and Breakfast on the Island,

and the next night at another B & B I know of in the U.P. in Curtis Michigan.

The couple agreed with her plans and Carl said, "I don't think we need a day to rest up. Let's play it by ear and plan on going after the bank, that way we won't have to rush getting back. It will give us another day."

"It sounds good to me, if that is all right with you, Hazel," Bertha said.

"I'll be ready," she smiled. "I can't wait to see what there is about this state that keeps people returning."

As they prepared to leave the restaurant, Jeff and his sister Jan came in. Stopping at their table, Bert introduced them to Carl and Hazel, telling them Jeff was Eric's builder.

"Are you moving to our city?" Jeff asked.

"Yes, we haven't really started looking for a house yet but plan to next week," Carl told him.

"Bert, why don't you show them the two new ones I'm finishing in Michaywe? One is a spec home but the other home is one I designed for a fellow that was transferred out of state. He was really upset he wasn't going to live in it and I promised I'd try to get it sold for him before I finish it. I think you might like it. He had excellent taste and spared no expense in having it built to his exact specifications. It is such a shame. I would like it myself, but I can't get my wife to move again."

"I don't blame her," Bert said. "I forgot how much trouble it is to get moved in and settled. We'll come by on Saturday if there will be someone there to give us a key. We're taking a trip north tomorrow."

Arrangements were made and Jan and Jeff left for their table. "He sure seems like a nice guy," Carl commented.

"He is, and very honest. He will tell you what the house will cost and won't play games at the closing. If you make any changes he signs them and you sign them and at the closing you will know exactly how much the home will cost you," Bertha said.

"The last time we built a house it ran me ten thousand more then the builders estimate. He moved a door he had mistakenly put in the wrong place and tried to charge us two hundred dollars for moving it back to where it belonged," Carl said. "That is when we decided never to build again but it sounds like his houses are almost finished. I would like to take a look at them."

"Why don't we go in the morning before leaving town," Hazel suggested.

On the way out of the dining room, Bert stopped by Jan and Jeff's table and told them they would be there first thing in the morning to pick up a key.

Jeff smiled at her, "Don't bother coming all the way into town. I have keys hidden; the same place we hid yours. Help yourself," he smiled

.   Bert thanked him and took the couple home.

They sat and talked until nine and then Carl and Hazel turned in for the night. "You're right. I have adjusted to the time change already," Carl smiled thanking her again for all she had done to make them feel welcome. "This has been more difficult for Hazel than for me," he said again, putting his arm around his wife. "She left her whole family back there. I'm hoping some may move here when they get tired of fighting all that traffic."

"Don't plan on it," Hazel told him. "I don't think any of them like snow."

"We will see. We sure adjusted in a hurry," He told his wife.

"Why shouldn't we. We both have good jobs; we're looking for a new house and have met several new friends; all within days of our arrival," Hazel said and reached for Bert's hand and squeezed it.

Bert smiled at the women. "I think I'll call it a day. You two stay and talk but I'm too tired. We have a lot to do tomorrow," she said, rising to go to bed.

Chapter Sixteen

The next morning Bert took them by each of the houses Jeff had suggested. The first did not look too interesting but Jeff was right; the second one was lovely. Bertha found the hidden key and inserted it in the lock, opening the door. The minute they walked in Bert knew Hazel wanted this house. "Don't you think we should look around a little more? We haven't talked to the bank yet to see if we can borrow enough to buy something like this."

Bert found a flyer describing the house lying on the cupboard and handed it to Carl. He took one look at the price and said, "I don't believe this. Honey, if you want it; it's yours. I know we can afford this much."

Bertha laughed, "I told you, you would be surprised what you can purchase in Michigan compared to where you came from."

"It's hard to believe. We had a small two bedroom condo we sold for more than this," Hazel said looking at the sheet Carl had given her. "I don't think we have to look any further. This is perfect. Jeff said we could be in within a month and I can still pick out the colors of the paint and carpet."

"Let's go on our trip and we can make up our mind while we are gone," Carl suggested.

"Honey, he may sell it while we're on the Island. Please let's at least go talk to him before we leave. He may have another buyer.

Furthermore, we don't know what the carpet allowance will be and maybe we will have to add to it. The bank will want to know all that," Hazel told him.

"Okay, we will stop on the way through town and talk to him," Carl smiled at her.

Bertha drove them over to Jeff's office, and was lucky enough to find him in.

They walked into his reception area and Jeff came out to meet them.

"Hello again, did you get a chance to see the houses?" he asked.

"We wouldn't be here if we had not stopped by this morning," Bertha smiled at him. "Mr. & Mrs. Senderson would like to talk to you if you have the time," Bertha said.

"Right this way," Jeff said, directing them to his office.

Bert stayed behind. She was talking to Jan an hour later when Carl asked her to come into Jeff's office. She walked in and joined them. "Jeff said we could be in the first or second week of next month. Will we wear out our welcome if we stay with you until the house is finished?" Carl asked.

"You know better than that. I'll enjoy the company," Bert told them. She did not like staying alone with Art roaming around. At least he had not called after she did not answer his luncheon invitation; maybe he finally gave up.

"We thought maybe you might be expecting your next renter," Hazel said.

"No, he won't be moving in until January, and the kids won't be here before Christmas, so that gives you plenty of time," she assured her.

"The gentleman that just left Jeff's office was a mortgage rep from the local bank," Carl explained to Bertha. "He was here taking an application in the adjoining office and Jeff called him in here. He took our application for the loan, and said he will have it processed in plenty of time to close. He promised us the lowest rate anywhere, and we said we were sure you would make sure of that," He smiled at Bert.

"That's wonderful. You didn't take very long making up your mind," Bert told them.

"We figure if Jeff did such a good job on your place and was building our boss's house; we won't be disappointed with it when Jeff finished ours. We did increase the carpet allowance, just in case we can't find what we want at a lesser price. Jeff said you know where to go to get the best carpet prices. The mortgage man said we could always apply any money left over toward something else that might come up. If you can give us a couple more minutes we would like to get the paper work done," Hazel said.

"Don't worry about the paper work. It will take more than a few minutes. Why don't you go on your trip and stop in Monday. I can have everything ready for your signatures, and in the mean time, I'll see if I can get the bank to hurry even faster on your mortgage," Jeff suggested.

Carl got out his checkbook to give Jeff a deposit. Jeff stopped him, "that won't be necessary. We will take the deposit when you come in to sign the papers."

"That is fine with us," Carl said and shook his hand. Jan came in, congratulated them on their new home, and walked with them out to the truck.

"If it is convenient for you, how would Monday be for our lunch date?" She asked Jan. "We are going to take off for up north and will be gone a couple days," Bertha told her as Jan walked them to the S.U.V.

Jan said Monday was fine and they said goodbye and Bert drove out of the office complex.

"I'm so excited. I don't know if I can wait until we get back to tell Mom we bought a house already," she told Carl.

"Here," he said and handed her his cell phone, "tell her there will be plenty of room for her and dad if they decide to come for a visit."

She called her mother and talked about the house for ten minutes. "I'll call you later when we get back. I'm on our cell phone. We are in Bertha's car and we're taking a trip to the U.P. That's the Upper Peninsula and an S.U.V. is a service utility vehicle," she laughed. She looked over at Carl and said, "She wondered what U.P. and S.U.V. meant. She thought I was talking another language," she laughed again. Disconnecting from her mother she smiled at Bert. "You've been wonderful. I don't know what we would do without you," she smiled.

"I'm happy to help," Bertha returned her smile.

Chapter Seventeen

They were driving through a canopy of trees and the sun shown on the leaves, turning them a beautiful golden color. They seemed to sparkle like so many diamonds. "I like the red leafed trees best, but they are all so lovely," Hazel said as Bertha drove into the state parking lot. They walked back to the walking bridge and looked out over the trees. The little stream that ran through the property was almost invisible. Hazel took dozens of pictures. "I have to send some of these pictures home to the folks," she declared. "It is impossible to describe how breathtaking it is up here. I just hope the camera does justice to the colors."

"By the time we get back the colors should be at their peak in Michaywe and you can take some shots of your property. Those maple trees on your lot will make a beautiful picture for Christmas cards," Bertha told her.

"What a wonderful idea. We can send them to all our friends and they can see our new home and how lovely it is here," she said smiling at her husband. He gave her a hug and smiled back at her. He was pleased she seemed so happy.

They went on to Curtis and stayed at the Inn on Lake Manistique. The food was excellent as usual and it was just chilly enough to have a fire in their stone fireplace. They sat before the fire after their meal and had their coffee. "I have to drink decaf for my health," Bert told them, "and it's a good thing because every time I have any caffeine this time of night it keeps me awake."

"I would like to go to bed. I'm tired; I'll probably sleep like a baby," Carl said, smiling, "but I'm afraid Hazel is so wound up she will be awake for hours yet."

"You go on up honey if you want. I'll join you shortly. I brought my night-light to read by and a good book. I'll try not to wake you," she smiled at her husband. "He could sleep through an earthquake once he nods off," She told Bert as he climbed the stairs. "I can lie next to him and read for hours and he won't know what time I came to bed."

"Jeff was the same way. I'm a lot like you. If I get six hours, I'm happy and if I got anymore than that, Jeff wanted to take my temperature. He knew I had to be coming down with something," Bertha laughed. "He actual slept through an earthquake one year while we were visiting Detroit. It wasn't a big one like we had in California but they say it shook Tiger Stadium. Bert found talking about Jeff was a little easier every day.

The next day it was still lovely and they drove on to Grand Maria's and stopped at Bertha's favorite little restaurant that looked like an old fashioned diner and ice-cream parlor. They ate Buffalo burgers. It was the first time Carl or Hazel had tried Buffalo and said they liked it better than hamburger; especially when they found out how little fat there was in buffalo compared to hamburger.

They drove around and found the B & B; stayed the night and then drove back down to Mackinaw.

They took the ferry over to the Island and took the carriage tour first, before renting bikes.

They enjoyed the tour but Bertha could see they liked the bike trail better. She took them to see her friend Joan, who lived on the Island. Joan took them by bike around the residential area. "We get used to riding bikes around here, as you can see there are no cars except for emergencies vehicles," she explained.

"Bertha warned us we would either do a lot of bike riding or walking. Fortunately we enjoy both," Carl told the woman.

As they were leaving Joan gave them a box of honey still in the cone, she had harvested herself. They thanked her and said their goodbyes. Carl and Hazel got on their bikes again and started down the hill, giving Bertha a little time alone with her friend.

Joan went over to Bert and gave her a big hug. "Nice kids," she said. "Honey, I was so sorry to hear about Jeff. Please, let's see more of one another."

"I'm finding out how hard it must have been for you these past ten years. At least I had a few extra years with Jeff. We will definitely see more of each other," she smiled at her friend. "Why don't you try to come to my place before you get frozen in?" Bert asked. She knew the lake would be frozen over in a couple of months and very little traffic came across from Mackinaw unless by snowmobile and that could get dangerous.

"I'm going to Florida this winter. I've bought a condo down there" she said and gave Bert a brief description of it. Bert knew where it was as she had seen the development many times while visiting Clearwater. "I decided to spend a few months of the winter there. It's gotten a little too quiet here lately, in the winter months. Less and less people are toughing out the really cold season. I'll call and let you know when I'll be leaving and stop at your place over night," Joan told her. "Why don't you go with me and spend some time down there? I have plenty of room."

"Thank you for the invitation, Joan. I might take you up on it some time but this winter I will be extremely busy. Carl and Hazel's boss has asked me to decorate his new office and get it set up, by the first of the year. But, keep the invitation open. Your place sounds perfect. I'll look forward to your visit, just call and let me know when. I have an answering service, so if I'm not there, leave a message. I'll be around town some where, and I'll call you back," Bert told her. She hugged her, waved, said goodbye, and mounted her bike and joined Carl and Hazel.

They took their bikes back to the rental company and boarded the next ferry.

It was a fast, quiet ride across. Each seemed to be enjoying the ride and watching the colors along the shorelines.

Getting back into Bertha's car Carl said. "Would you like me to drive?"

"If you don't mind, I will be able to watch the scenery better and we are only an hour from home," Bertha said and got out and walked around to the passenger seat. "Why don't you get in front Hazel; I like being chauffeured home," Bert laughed.

Hazel laughed and got into the front seat. Bert sat in the back seat, where she could not watch the driver but was able to talk easily to Hazel.

They chatted about all they had seen until they saw the Gaylord City exit sign. "Let's stop and see what they have accomplished at the building while we were gone," Hazel suggested.

Carl readily agreed and added, "Point out that restaurant you've been talking about, Bert. Then Hazel and I would like to take you there for lunch tomorrow. The place that has the great Greek Salad."

"You'll get no argument from me," Bert laughed, pointing it out to him before he drove to the building. He had learned his way around quickly. They would pick up their new cars the first of the week and he would have no difficulty going wherever he wanted.

They entered the office building and the transformation was astonishing. The workers were still there and working, none stop. The ugly wood was removed from the walls. They had the walls plastered and painted and were applying the final coat of trim.

"Wow! You have done one fine job in here," Bert complemented the men and made a mental note to see they were paid a nice bonus.

"We wanted to be out of here before you came back but we still have several hours more work before we're finished. The wood trim is taking a little longer than we anticipated. I started the wood around one of the windows and didn't like the first color so we sanded and re-did it. I don't think you can tell which one it is. This new stain looks much better," He told her.

"You're right. I can't tell you which one had to be re-sanded. Well, we will get out of your way and let you finish," Bert said and started to leave.

Hazel had been pacing off her office when Bert suggested they leave. She and Carl followed her out of the building. "They will get it done a lot faster without us around. They enjoy talking," Bertha smiled.

"The colors in the entree are beautiful," Hazel told her. "I can hardly wait until the new walls are completed in our offices, and we can move in the furniture."

"I'll get on them Monday dear, now let's go eat. I'm starved," He smiled at his wife. She looked at him and started to say something but he interrupted her, "Yes! I know. I'm always starved," and the three of them enjoyed the joke.

They pulled up in front of a little restaurant attached to a motel that sat just off the freeway. They only wanted a light meal and would have the Greek Salads tomorrow.

Carl said, "We could have walked."

"You might have been able to but I can still feel my legs pumping those bike petals," Hazel smiled at him.

"I'm with you," Bert heartily agreed.

Returning home, Carl and Hazel retired to the lower level and after Bert got her e-mail off the computer, she went to bed.

Arthur had finely stopped calling all together and she had not seen him walk by the house in several days. Her nerves were beginning to settle down. She slept well that night with guests just below her.

The next day they had a light breakfast and headed for the office. Some of the men were still there working, so Bert took them shopping and later they went to the restaurant Carl and Hazel wanted to try.

When they walked into the establishment, the owner's daughter greeted them with a smile and said, "Good to see you back. I heard you were moving up here for good. We were sorry to hear about Jeff," she told Bert and showed them to a booth that had just been vacated. "I'll be right back and take your order."

"Do you know everyone in town?" Hazel asked.

"No, but Jeff and I spent a lot of time here. She only just returned herself from California that's why she sports that great tan," Bertha told them. "They have the best soups in town. I recommend any soup on the menu. They make them all up fresh daily and they are terrific. I wish I knew how they do it day after day. Some day I may find one I don't like, if I live long enough,"

Bert smiled. "Oh! They have my favorite today." She was going to order a take out of the potato soup for her evening snack.

They all ordered a cup of the potato soup and a Greek salad placed over potato salad. Bert said it was the only way to enjoy a Greek Salad. Both women needed take home boxes and Carl ordered a sandwich to go.

"That takes care of this evening," he smiled. "Now no one has to cook."

"Sounds good to me," both women laughed.

Arriving home Carl and Hazel retired to the lower level for a well deserved nap and Bertha went to her room, turned on the television and was surprised when she fell asleep, waking two hours later. Warming up her soup, she ate the entire amount. She was going to save some for later but she found she was far hungrier then she thought.

Carl and Hazel must have gone for an evening walk as it was quite late when she heard them return. They were so quiet she hardly knew they had come into the house but she heard Carl put the security system on for the night.

Chapter Eighteen

That Monday the three headed for the new office building. They worked throughout the day and were able to get all the lumber Carl needed stacked in the rooms he would be using it in. The big job was moving it up the stairs to the second floor. The only offices that would be on the second floor were Eric's private office and that of Hazel, his secretary. He wanted his furnishings in mahogany and Bert knew she would have a tough time finding the mahogany furniture he needed. Hazel's office was much easier. She wanted oak and finding her office furniture was not difficult. In Michigan, you could find Oak office furniture almost anywhere.

By the end of the week, Carl and Bertha had all the mahogany walls up in Eric's office and Hazel ran around cleaning up as fast as they made a mess. The three worked very well together and Carl was pleased to see Bertha knew how to work along side him. It made it a lot easier and the walls seemed to fly up. They were not going to finish the trim until after they had the walls in Hazel's office completed; then Carl would finish the rooms while Hazel and Bertha went to

Traverse City on a buying binge.

Carl wanted to be finished before they left for their Thanksgiving Holiday.

Hazel and Bert tried to find the office equipment in town but could not find everything they needed so they figured Traverse City was the closest place that might carry what they were looking for.

Bertha hired a local company to make the window coverings. They were to meet with the Drapery Company as soon as the finishing of the window trim was complete.

"I for one am going to call it a day," Bertha told the two. "I think we have all done enough for this week. Let's go home, shower and go to dinner; my treat."

"That's an offer we can't refuse," Hazel told her. "Come on Carl, the work isn't going to run away, let's split. After the weekend off, you will be ready to do battle with the finishing work on Monday," she smiled.

"You'll get no argument from me. I was afraid Bertha couldn't keep up with me but I found I was the one having difficulties," Carl smiled at his wife, took off his nail apron dropped it on the clean floor and followed the two women down the stairs.

Arriving back at the house, Bertha went into her den and found a message from Eric on her answering service. He was not going to be able to get back for Thanksgiving and hoped everyone would come out there. He would definitely be in Michigan for Christmas and expected a big holiday meal from his sister. He said she had invited the three of them and hoped they could make it.

Bert called Elizabeth to find out if they would be up for Christmas before calling Eric's sister. Elizabeth and her husband were planning to come the day after Christmas. They had promised Max's folks they would spend the Holiday with them. Bert did not really care. She had enough people around her to keep her happy until Elizabeth and Max arrived. She was going to drive down next week and spend Thanksgiving with them anyway. That would still give her time to get all the gifts wrapped. She usually had them bought and wrapped by Thanksgiving but she was running behind. She talked to Carl and Hazel and then called Mary accepting her invitation for the three of them.

Carl and Hazel were leaving the following week for California to be with Hazel's parents and family members for Thanksgiving dinner. Mary and Steve would be seeing Eric and their families in California, but were flying out the day after Hazel and Carl. Bertha offered to drive them all to Detroit so they could fly from there but they wanted to fly out of Petoskey. Bertha was relieved. She did not want to spend a week down state and would have had to if they had taken her up on her offer.

Now that all the plans had been made for their holiday, Bert and Hazel left for their shopping trip on Monday. They had lunch at Bert's favorite restaurant and coffee in the mall.

They shopped until they were ready to drop. When they were finished they had purchased a lovely, plank topped desk with a matching two-drawer cadenza with sliding doors, for Eric's office. The four matching client chairs in Mahogany were in the same wine colored leather. Eric wanted wine for the accessories in his room. They found a large computer armoire to go on the wall beside his desk. The only thing Bert had wanted and could not find was a couple free standing, desk height, file cabinets in mahogany.

Hazel was thrilled with her new large oak desk with all its drawers. Her cadenza was larger then Eric's and would take up one whole wall in her office.

They told her they would have to order the mahogany furnishings but could deliver it all the week after Thanksgiving. Bertha told them not to hurry, as Carl wanted to be there when it arrived and he would not be returning until six days after Thanksgiving. Everything was set and the two ladies left the store, arm in arm and headed for Bert's car.

"I am so happy," Hazel said. "We did a good days work today. I can't believe we found everything for my office. I'm only sorry we couldn't find the cabinets you wanted for Eric's office."

"Oh, it's no problem. Carl and I can make them in my shop. That is why I wanted a wood sample from the desk. We can build them the size he wants and stain them to match the remainder of the furnishings," Bert told her.

"I'm sure Carl will want to help. If you don't mind a man in your workshop," Hazel smiled.

"He is welcome in my shop any time," Bert smiled back.

The two women went back home but stopped at the office on the way. It was amazing how much Carl had done while they were out enjoying themselves. They walked in and found him sweeping the scraps down the stairwell.

"Typical male. Couldn't you find the dust pan?" His wife asked.

"I was going to find it after I got it all downstairs," he laughed.

"I'll bet," Hazel said. "Here give me that and get cleaned up, we are going to dinner. I'll finish this."

Bert smiled at the two. They so enjoyed teasing one another. She found the dustpan and brought it over to Hazel. Bert held the handle, while Hazel filled the pan and then placed the scraps from the dustpan in the waiting trash barrel. By the time Carl had washed up, the women had finished cleaning where Carl had left off.

Hazel rode with Carl in his new S.U.V. truck and Bertha followed in hers. Bertha referred to hers as a car but in reality, it was a truck. They went to the local restaurant and afterward went home for a quiet evening.

Chapter Nineteen

Bertha turned the key in the lock and heard her security system turn on. She went into the laundry room and turned it to "stay". The house was quiet and had the feeling of being closed for several days. She went into the living room and started the fireplace, walked back down the hall and entered her bedroom. Everything was clean, as she had cleaned house before going down state. It was so nice to come home to a clean home. She changed into her pajamas, went to the kitchen, poured herself a Decaf Pepsi, and walked back into the living room. She sat in her favorite chair and turned on the television. It was too quiet; she needed the noise. It would take her a few days to get used to the stillness in the house, but she knew Carl and Hazel would be back in a couple days and everything would get back to normal. Tomorrow she would go check out the office and call the furniture movers. She tried to watch the program that was on the screen but got bored with it and turned on the news. As soon as the news was off, she went to bed, hoping she did not hear from Art tomorrow. At least he had stopped watching the house;

anyway she thought he had.

The next morning Bert left before nine o'clock and went downtown to have breakfast at the restaurant near the office. The daughter of the owner greeted her as usual, and they had a nice chat before her meal came. It was one of the few times they were not busy. In another two hours there would be a crowd in the hall and out onto the sidewalk, waiting to get in. She had a wonderful omelet and ordered soup to go. She would have it for lunch while she waited for the Drapery Company.

Walking out to the car, she ran into two friends she had not seen since her return. They talked for a while and Bert promised to keep in touch and drove to the office. It was after ten when she walked into the building. She locked the door behind her just in case she received an unwanted guest.

The smell of new wood was still in the air and it made her feel comfortable. She did not think she would ever tire of the smell of fresh wood; it reminded her of Jeff.

Greta arrived with the new window treatments an hour later. Bertha went over and unlocked the door. Greta and her assistant got busy installing the window treatments in the main reception area first. The two women worked for over three hours and told Bert they would be back after lunch. "We will bring the upstairs drapes later. I didn't want them to get messed up while we installed the lobby lavalieres. I didn't have room for everything in one load without getting them wrinkled," Greta explained to Bertha and left.

After locking the door, Bert sat in the back room and ate her soup. She was just finishing when Eric called. "How did you know where to find me?" she asked him.

"I knew if you weren't home, you would be down at the office. Lady, don't you ever take any time off?" he scolded her.

"What are you talking about? I took four days off when I went down state; that was enough," she laughed. "I want to get everything ready for the furniture. It should be here the day after Hazel and Carl return. I wanted to pick them up at the airport but your sister and her husband are arriving the same day, so they are driving back together. I have really missed them. I'll be glad to see them all. They are such nice couples."

"Yes! I am fortunate to have Hazel for a secretary. I had no choice on the sister but I couldn't have chosen a better one," Eric laughed.

"You're right there. Did you have a nice Holiday?" Bert asked.

"It was very nice. The only thing that would have made it nicer was if you could have been here, but we will have an even nicer Christmas. My folks have agreed to try to come out after Christmas. They are dying to see my new real estate purchases. Dad has to be sure they are doing everything right," He laughed.

"Don't worry there is plenty of room in your apartment," Bert told him.

"I can't impose on you with my folks too," Eric said.

"You most certainly can, if you want. Elizabeth is coming up the day after Christmas and she and Max can use the guestroom on the main floor. They usually stay there anyway, and will probably only be here a couple days." Bert informed him. "I would love to have them, but I imagine your sister would be put out if they didn't stay with her."

"I think she will have a house full too" Eric told her. "Max has asked his family to come for Christmas. We should have quite a crowd."

"It sounds wonderful. Carl, Hazel, and I have already accepted your sister's invitation," she told him. "Well friend, as soon as the drapery company finishes, I am going home and hit the sack. It has been a long day."

"Good night Schlick. I can't wait to see all that you have done. I bet I will love everything," he said.

"Is that the only reason you want to return?" Bert teased him and was sorry she said it, right after it came out of her mouth.

Of course, he caught it right away and laughed, "You know I want to see you more than the new office," He told her.

"It will be ready for you when you arrive," she said. "Everything is taking shape and looks like a distinguished Detective Agency," Bertha said, trying to change the subject.

"Okay," he said, knowing he should not push it any further. "See you soon. Give my best to everyone and tell our hostess at the club, we will be in for dinner the night I fly back," he said, and he must have been smiling when he hung up the phone; she could hear it in his voice.

Chapter Twenty

Eric pulled into Bert's driveway the week before he was expected. He did not stop at his new office. He wanted Bert to show it to him. Pulling a small U-Haul, he backed it into the small space off the front drive that Bert used to park her R.V. He noted she had already put her R.V. in storage for the winter. Getting out of his car, he went to the front door and rang the bell. No one answered so he used his key.

"Anyone home" he called out several times and then heard the security system buzzing. He went in and turned it off. Walked back to his car and brought in his luggage. It took him almost two hours to unload the U-Haul and put his stuff in the now vacant exercise room. He reset the alarm system, went back out to his car, and drove it to town to drop off the U-Haul at the local dealer. He stopped at K-Mart; purchased several shaving items he would need and went to men's store before heading back to Bert's.

When he arrived back at Bert's, she had still not returned, so he went downstairs to his new digs. He needed a shower. He went in and turned the shower on as hot as he thought he could stand it and got under the cascading water. After several minutes, he got out, wrapped a large towel around himself, and went into the living room area. Turning on the T. V. he put his feet up on the coffee table and leaned back against the quilt that was hung over the back of the leather couch. He would rest a few minutes before getting dressed. An hour later, he awoke, thinking he heard noises. He turned off the television and listened. He was sure he had heard Bertha come in. He went to the foot of the stairs and yelled up, "is that you, Schlick?"

Bertha went to the top of the stairs and yelled down, "Yes, is that you Eric? What a pleasant surprise to find you here. Why don't you come up and I'll fix us a snack." She was so happy to have him back.

"Give me ten minutes and I'll be up," he called back. He walked into his bedroom and put on clean underwear, socks, a bulky knit sweater and corduroy slacks. Bert had told him she liked him in cords. He hoped she liked the new sweater he purchased in town, to wear with them. He would have to get her to take him shopping for a winter wardrobe before it really got cold. He did not have too many warm clothes and about froze the last two days of his trip. He was all right as long as he stayed in his car where it was warm, but whenever he stopped to have lunch or to stay at a motel, he had to run from the car to the buildings or freeze in his tracks. This was the last time he would take the northern route through North Dakota to get to his new home. He disliked mornings the most because he had to wait for the car heater to catch up. He reminded himself to get an attachment on his car to start it in the morning without having to go outside. He noticed Bertha had one on both her vehicles.

He was smiling when he came up the stairs. Bertha noticed his lovely smile again and returned his smile. She also noted how handsome he looked in his cords and a lovely sweater she had not seen before. "New?" she asked.

"Yes, I bought it in town at the men's store you told me about. I wondered if you would mind going shopping with me some time soon. I don't have any other warm clothes and could use some help picking out what I'll need," Eric said.

"I'd love too. We could go to Traverse City's big mall. They have several fine men's shops. Let's plan on it this weekend. Maybe Mary and Steve would like to join us."

They sat and had coffee and a few crackers with spinach dip. "I want this recipe, this is great."

Bert smiled, "I probably shouldn't tell you but I get it the same place I get this coffee. If you want, we can pick up both when we go to Traverse. Have you seen your sister yet?" Bert asked.

"No and I haven't even been to the new office yet," Eric told her.

"You haven't," Bert said in astonishment." Well, drink up. We are going to the office. You better get a coat."

"I don't have one yet," Eric told her.

"Just a minute," Bert said and went downstairs to her walk-in cedar closet. She returned carrying a down-filled car coat. "Try this on. I kept it in case someone needed a good winter coat. Jeff was about your size. It may be a little large, he was a little heavier," she smiled at Eric.

He thanked her and put the coat on. It fit perfectly. "I'll borrow it until I get to Traverse City and pick up one, if you don't mind," Eric told her.

"Keep it, please. I've been meaning to get rid of some of Jeff's winter things anyway. If you wouldn't mind wearing some of his clothes, we could go down later and see what you might want. There are some we bought on our last trip and he hadn't had the chance to wear them," Bert suggested.

"Sure; if it wouldn't bother you, having someone else wear his clothes," Eric said.

"Of course not. I would rather see them being used than to give them to someone that wouldn't appreciate them. He had several very nice sweaters, I am sure you could wear."

They walked out to Bert's car and she tossed the keys to Eric. "We better stop at Mary's and tell her you're back," Bert said. "We can find out if they are available this weekend."

Eric drove the short distance to his sister's home and she came running out to greet them. "Get a coat on, silly," He told her. "You'll catch your death in this weather."

"What do you mean? This is a heat spell we are having. I just hope it snows again before Christmas," she teased him. "Wait for another month. Then you can say it is cold."

"It doesn't get that bad," Bert interjected. "It is warmer up here than it is down state. We have a much dryer season." She told Eric and Mary laughed. Eric did not know which one to believe.

They went into the house and Steve walked over and shook Eric's hand. "It's about time you stopped in. Your sister has been having a snit-fit. She saw your car there several hours ago," Steve told Eric.

"I took a shower and made the mistake of setting down. I fell asleep for over an hour and would probably still be sawing wood if Bert had not come home. It was a pretty boring, cold trip, with no one to talk to," Eric told his brother-in-law.

"Well you're here safe and sound. That is all that matters," Steve told him. "Have you seen the office? Carl and Hazel are probably still there. You can't pull them away even with an offer of a free meal," Steve laughed.

"That sounds serious. We were headed down there next. Would you two like to come along and go to dinner afterward," Bertha asked.

Steve saw the frown on Eric and said, "Thanks but we already have plans. We'll take a rain check for tomorrow evening if you want to go out."

"We were going to go to Traverse City tomorrow for the day, and wondered if you both would like to join us," Eric said.

"Sounds good," Mary answered for both of them. "I have no idea what Steve has planned for tonight but it better be good." She looked at Steve and he gave her a smile that said, can't you see Eric would like dinner alone with Bert tonight. She smiled and waited until Eric and Bert left before saying to Steve. "You caught that faster than I did, dear. I'm going to have to pay more attention next time. I have never had to share Eric before," she said, and she was not at all sure she wanted too, but if she wanted him happy, she had better get used to it.

Chapter Twenty-one

They arrived at the new office building as Carl and Hazel was preparing to drive away. They spotted Bert's car and walked over to find Eric behind the wheel. "Hey boss, you're here. You ready to go to work?" she asked. "I figured you'd be showing up pretty soon. There are a dozen faxes waiting for you."

"See! She is a slave driver," Eric said to Bert. "Now you know why I keep her around."

"Come on in. You won't believe what these two ladies have done," Carl said proudly.

Eric was more than happy with the reception area and told them as much. When he went to his private office, he was astonished. "How did you find all this furniture?" He asked.

"Carl and Bertha went out to Bert's workshop and built anything they couldn't find," Hazel told him.

"Well, I couldn't be more satisfied. This is absolutely beautiful. I can't believe all you have accomplished in a couple months. Let's look at your office, Hazel. Do you like it?" He asked as they walked across the hall.

"What's not to like," she said. "This is exactly what I wanted."

"It is lovely. Look at all the oak files. Very impressive," Eric said. "Now if we can fill them up, we will be in business."

"You would be surprised how many are already filled," Hazel told him. "We have several inquires for your services, and I've transferred the California files on discs so you can keep up with them."

"That's fine, but the first case I want started is Nancy Plant, Bert's friend. We can get started on it Monday. I want you two to take a couple days off. It looks like you haven't for quite awhile."

"We only finished today. Bert is as bad as we are about working. She was here until late this afternoon, putting the finishing touches in your office," she told him. "She also makes a good receptionist. Until we can hire a full time lady, she has been helping out. I have interviewed a half dozen people so far but haven't found the right one yet."

"I'll see she takes some time off too. Now let's lock up and come back Monday," Eric suggested and took Bert's arm, steering her toward the stairway.

They walked down and out of the office building. Getting into their individual cars, Carl and Hazel waved and drove off. Eric helped Bert into the car and said, "They bought matching S.U.V.'s."

"Yes, she said they were always going different places and he was hauling lumber and junk in his and she wasn't going to let him do that in her new truck," Bert laughed.

"I need to get me one of those before too long. I don't want to drive my Lincoln, in bad weather. It was bad enough coming across country pulling that U-Haul. Did they get their vehicles in town?" he asked.

"Yes, we were able to get fleet prices through your company, on both of them. Hazel set it up with the local dealer for you too; just in-case you wanted to get a truck when you got here."

"She is always way ahead of me. I was really pleased they agreed to move here," Eric said.

"She said they couldn't afford not to. You made it too appealing. After they bought their home and moved in, I don't think you could get them to transfer back," Bert told him.

Eric drove to a new restaurant they had wanted to try. He dropped her off at the door. "I can walk back with you," She said, noticing he would have to park at the back of the lot. There was a large crowd dining tonight.

"No reason for both of us to get cold," he smiled at her, leaning over and opening her door.

She thanked him and got out. Bertha was glad he had dropped her off. They had one booth left and she told them she wanted it and would wait for her other party. The hostess assured her she would show him back to her table. She smiled and followed the girl to a small, secluded booth on the left wall of the restaurant. She had not finished looking at the menu, when Eric was shown to her table.

"I see you found your way," Bert smiled. "With the waiting line in the lobby, I didn't know how they would know which person was the one I was waiting for." Bert laughed, "She even knew it would be a man. That girl is wasted here. She really knows people."

"Not really; I described you to her when I entered," he laughed. "But maybe we should see if she wants to interview as a receptionist."

They both ordered the house special. Prime rib so big it covered the large plates. Bertha took over half of hers home. The red potatoes were finished off in garlic butter. They agreed to both dine on the garlic, so they would not stink each other out of the car on the way home. They did not have horseradish sauce so Bert ordered sour cream and horseradish. She mixed it together to make a nice sauce for her and Eric. They did not bother having deserts, they were both too full. Eric insisted on paying the bill, and Bertha thanked him.

"After all you've done, a meal is cheap pay," He told her.

"Wait till you see my bill," she laughed.

"Whatever it is; it will be worth it," Eric told her.

She did not intend to send him a bill. She enjoyed doing it. If Eric found out Nancy's death was either suicide or murder, Bert's work had been worthwhile. The look on her face must have turned sad as Eric said, "A penny for your thoughts."

"They wouldn't be worth a penny," Bert smiled. "I just got to thinking about Nancy again. What a waste."

"Well, we will get on it first thing Monday. Don't worry, we will find out what really happened to her. Now let's try to enjoy ourselves over the weekend and worry about work Monday," Eric suggested

.   Bert agreed. "That sounds like a good idea. How about going home and calling Mary to see if they will come over and I'll fix us some cappuccino."   She knew his sister wanted to spend some time with him, his first evening back.

"Okay! If they returned from their appointment," Eric said and called on his cell phone.

Mary answered and Eric said, "You're home already! Bert would like to know if you would like to come by in about an hour and she will fix cappuccino."

"You sure you don't mind," she teased her brother.

"Don't be smart. You coming or not?" Eric laughed.

She laughed in return and said, "We'd love to come." She hung up the phone and told Steve they were invited over to Bert's home.

Mary and Steve went over an hour later and were greeted by her brother. "We went to the new office. Have you seen it?" he asked her.

"Yes!" Steve said. "i couldn't keep old nosy away. She was dying to see it and kept hounding me until I went with her."

"Don't listen to him," Mary laughed. "He wanted to see it as bad as I did. We were very impressed"

"So was I," Eric laughed.

They had a nice evening together chatting about their trip that weekend. Around ten Mary and Steve excused themselves and headed for home. "I think I'll call it a day too," Eric said. "I'm bushed," and he retired to the lower level.

Chapter Twenty-two

Eric and Bertha picked up Mary and Steve the next morning and they headed for Traverse City. "I'd like to go to the discount house first, if you two don't mind," Bertha told Mary and Steve.

"No! I want to get a card so we can shop there too," Mary said.

"You could use mine but they put your picture on it. Let me get one for you, using mine. It will cost you a lot less," Bertha told her.

"Can you get me one too?" Eric asked.

"Sure! We will get them at the welcome desk before we start shopping," Bert told him and that is what they did.

After they got their cards, Bert headed for the coffee and Mary went to the house wares department. Eric and Steve pushed a cart to the office equipment department and loaded four large boxes of copy paper into the cart.

Steve laughed. "I better get another cart if you are purchasing anything else.

"Good idea. As long as I'm here I might as well get the stuff Hazel has on this list," he said to Steve.

The men caught up with Bert and Mary as they started to get in line to check out. Both the women's carts were also pilled high.

"Did you buy out the place?" Steve asked his wife. "It looks like you have enough food there to feed an army."

"I only purchased what I needed," she smiled at her husband. "I got some of that spinach anchovy dip that Eric was telling us about. If you're not good I won't give you any," she teased him.

Returning to the car, Bert put all the perishables in the cooler she had placed in the back of the vehicle. There was enough ice inside the cooler to last several hours. They headed for the large mall they had passed on the way in. Bert and Eric parted from the other couple and made a date to return to the Ferris wheel in two hours. The mall had a beautiful Ferris wheel inside the main lobby, and would be good place for them to meet.

Eric found several sweaters, three pair of trousers, two hats and a beautiful topcoat, all in an hour and a half. Bert felt as though her legs were ready to fall off. He shopped just as she did. Get in, find, pay for it and move on to another store. They stopped on the way back to the Ferris wheel and made another purchase for Eric; two pair of boots; one for good and a pair for deep snow. Jeff's boots were the only thing that would not fit Eric. Eric had larger feet. He did take several new sweaters and some cords Jeff had left behind. The remainder of Jeff's clothes, she and Eric delivered to a family that could use them. Eric felt he should now be prepared for any kind of cold weather, his sisters or Bertha's

They beat Mary and Steve back to the Ferris wheel, and were enjoying a diet coke as they waited for them, but they did not have long to wait.

"How in the world did you buy all this in so little time?" Mary laughed.

"Schlick shops like I do," He said.

"Say no more," his sister laughed. She turned to Bert and said, "I refused to shop with him after the last time. My legs felt like they were going to fall off. I like to take my time."

Bert smiled and led them back to the parking lot. They stopped next at the snowmobile dealer in Gaylord where Eric picked out a pair of moon boots. "I need an outfit too,' He said.

"Yes, but let's get you a good helmet first," Bert suggested. "Try this one on for size," she said handing him a black helmet with an attached shield and nose guard.

"It fits fine, but it's terribly expensive. It cost four times what the boots cost," he said.

"Yes, but believe me, you need a good helmet," Bert told him and his sister agreed.

"She is right. You can go cheaper on a helmet but that one is a good one," Mary told him.

"Now I need an outfit; what one do you recommend," He asked Steve.

"Well the leather is sharp looking, but for warmth I'd get this one," Steve told him. "It has bib overalls and a long jacket."

"Okay, let's find one in my size," Eric said and the men finely found one that fit Eric. He went over and paid for his purchases and Steve helped him get them all out to the car.

When they arrived in Michaywe' they all agreed none of them wanted to cook so they drove directly to the club.

The hostess gushed all over Eric and told him how pleased she was to see him back. He thanked her politely, put his arm around Bertha's shoulder, and walked her to their table.

"Did the big bad women scare you," his sister teased him. Steve and Mary noticed how he put his arm around Bert and the three of them laughed.

"Well if she didn't take the hint this time brother dear, she never will," she continued to tease him. "You made it pretty obvious you belong to Bert."

"I hope she doesn't spread around a bunch of rumors. He is staying at your place," Steve said.

"I'm sorry Schlick. I never thought."

"Don't worry about it. I could take a few rumors once in a while. It will give the gossips someone else to pick on," Bert laughed.

"You are a good sport," Eric smiled that beautiful smile that she could not resist.

They made it an early evening, as everyone was tired from their busy day.

Eric put on the security system before returning to his apartment and Bert said goodnight and went to her room.

She watched a little T.V. and fell asleep with it still on. It shut off automatically two hours later.

Chapter Twenty-three

Bertha had asked Eric, Mary and Steve to go to church on Sunday with her and she introduced them around, and after the service, they had lunch with her usual church friends.

Eric wanted to stop at his office after lunch so he and Bertha drove one car and Steve and Mary followed them to the restaurant. When they were through eating, Steve and Mary went home, but Eric and Bert headed for his office.

Eric was anxious to get started on Nancy's death. He needed to get Bertha to tell him everything she knew about Nancy and her husband and he figured she would be more open if they were alone at the office. He was right. She told of the beatings and of the many times that Nancy had used the excuse that she ran into furniture when she showed up at card parties with several bruises.

"Everyone knew that snake had hit her again. I could never figure out why she put up with it. I think there must have been something in her past he held over her head; that was the only explanation I could think of," Bertha told him.

"It sounds like a good place to start would be about twenty years ago. You said she was only married about twelve years, when you met her?" Eric asked.

"Yes and I don't think he started his brutality until about eight years into the marriage. From what I understood; everything was like a honeymoon for the first few years until they moved back here and then it steadily went from bad to worse," Bert told him.

"What do you think she was trying to hide?" Eric asked. He knew there was something that Bert was reluctant to tell him.

Bertha hesitated and then added, "I think she must have had a child at some time. She would get all teary eyed when a child came into a room and tried to set next to her."

"Okay, we will check birth records for the five years before and after she married Arthur," He told her. "Can you think of anything else?" he asked.

"I know she was born in Indiana because we talked about both of us being born in Ft. Wayne. Is any of this helping?" Bert asked.

He smiled at her. "You have provided us with several leads to follow up. I guess that is enough for today. I just noticed the time. I've been asking questions for two hours. Time for us to call it a halt for now. You have been a big help," Eric told her. "Do you want to come with me tomorrow and handle the phones?" He asked. "Hazel informed me you seemed to enjoy it and it would relieve her while she interviews receptionist applications. I'll spring for lunch," he laughed.

"I'd love to. I have all my Christmas shopping done and only have to wrap a few more gifts. I can do that in the evening," Bert told her.

Eric walked outside behind her, turned and locked the door. He opened her car door and said, "Sometime Monday you will have to take me to the car dealer. I would like to get an S.U.V. just like yours." He pulled away from the curb and headed toward Bert's home as she directed him in a different way to get to her house. "I like this back way better," he commented. "It seems much closer."

"It isn't, but it is faster." Bert told him. "There are not as many curves and hills. They arrived at the house and Eric asked if she would like to make some coffee. "I'll be happy to. We can watch what is left of the Lyon's game," Bert told him.

"You're still a fan?" Eric laughed.

"Yes! You wait and see, they will turn things around; now that they have a good coach and a new quarterback," she smiled.

They watched the game and Bert was able to make Eric eat crow. The Lyons won and was four and two so far for the season. Not great, but better then they had been in the past. They had a great defensive team now and the offense was improving every game.

They made plans for the following day and Eric went down to the lower level.

Bertha retired to her room and had a very difficult time getting comfortable. Her mind kept racing over the day and all she had told Eric. She hoped she had not missed anything. It was after two a.m. when she turned off the television and forced herself to concentrate on going to sleep.

Chapter Twenty-four

Monday morning, Bertha dressed in one of her best pantsuits; taking extra care on her make-up. She smiled at her reflection in the mirror. Not too bad, old girl, she said and laughed at herself. She knew she looked her best when she walked out of her room.

Eric had left early and she was to be at the office at nine o'clock. Drinking a quick cup of coffee and munching on a bagel, she went out to her car. She arrived at the office as Hazel was unlocking it for the morning. Eric was up in his office and had locked the door so he would not be disturbed.

Hazel went up the stairs and said, "Hi boss! What are you doing here so early? Are we going to have new hours?"

"No, I wanted to get a head start on some things. I have been faxing our office in California the past hour. They have been working all night and I just sent them home. Those guys out there never know when to quit. It is only six o'clock there. I received some interesting news on Bertha's friend Nancy's husband though. It seems our man Art has a past," He told her.

Bertha was at the receptionists' desk when the young girl from the restaurant came in. She greeted her with a smile and said, "I'm so glad you decided to come in for an interview. I'll call Mrs. Senderson. Please sit down, she shouldn't be long." Bert buzzed Hazel's office and when she did not answer, she rang Eric. When he answered she asked, "Is Mrs. Senderson available. She has a young lady here for her nine thirty interview."

"She will be down in a few minutes. Please ask her to have a seat," Eric said.

The young woman sat on one of the new client chairs Bertha had strategically placed in the reception room. She seated herself so she could watch what Bert was doing. Several phone calls came in before Hazel appeared at the top of the staircase. She walked down and introduced herself to the young lady. "I understand my boss met you at a restaurant. He had high praise for your abilities in reading people." Hazel said smiling at the girl.

"It was not too difficult to place him with your receptionist. They were about the same age and equally as polite. I sometimes get some real bossy customers, and that night was one of them," she said.

"Well, let's go upstairs and talk. We won't be disturbed in my office. Katherine Morrison?" Hazel asked looking at the name on the application.

"Yes, but please call me Kathy."

The two women climbed the stairs and the interview lasted a good half-hour. When they

143

emerged Hazel preceded Kathy down the stairs and said, "Mrs. Schlinkenmayer, I'd like Kathy to handle the phones for a few minutes. Would you please show her what the number of buttons, stand for."

"I don't think that is necessary," Kathy said. "I was watching Mrs. Schlinkenmayer very closely and I think I can handle it."

Bert smiled at Kathy and moved from behind the large half moon shaped desk, making room for Kathy to sit before the phones. "She types adequately and knows her way around a computer. I want to hear how she sounds on the phone," Hazel explained.

Kathy's first phone request was to have Mrs. Schlinkenmayer go up to Hazel's office. Kathy answered several calls the same way she had heard Bertha answer them. Her voice was pleasant and when several calls came in at the same time she did not seem to be rattled. Most of the calls were from people trying to sell something to the new office in town. The others were for donations and two were for Eric.

A half-hour later Hazel appeared again and told her, she had the job. She said she realized Kathy could not start for at least two weeks and she had already asked Bert to fill in until then. Over the Holidays, they did not plan to be very busy; their Grand Opening day would not be until January second.

Kathy seemed happy she had the new employment. Her salary would be almost double and the benefit package was better than she had seen anywhere else. When Bertha appeared again, Kathy asked where she had purchased her pantsuit. "I have some nice clothes but I would like to purchase some more business oriented attire. You look so professional Mrs. Schlinkenmayer."

"Thank you Kathy. Please call me Bertha or Bert; everyone does. I'm afraid I purchased this suit in California but there is a store in Traverse City that carries the same brand. Let me write it down for you," Bert said picking up a pad of paper and pencil, she started writing. She handed the girl the slip of paper with the brand name and store name in the Traverse City Plaza. "They are a little high priced but not as bad as the store I bought my outfit from. I have shopped there several times and they are most helpful if you tell them what you want they bend over backward to accommodate you."

"I have Saturday off this week so I'll make a trip over there. Thank you so much. You have all been most helpful, and made me feel very comfortable," Kathy told her and left the building.

"I think we have a winner in that young lady," Hazel said walking down the stairs after Kathy had left. She had gone back upstairs to tell Eric they wanted to go to lunch.

"I think you're right. She did a great job on the phones, and it is apparent she wants to improve her position in life. She also gave me a compliment, and that never hurts," Bertha laughed.

"Yes, she is a pretty sharp young lady. Now, how about some lunch. Eric said we could switch the phones to his cell phone. We don't expect many visitors yet. I'd like to get one of those Greek Salads," Hazel smiled.

"They are addicting aren't they. Is Eric joining us?" Bert asked.

"We couldn't stop him if we tried," Hazel laughed.

"What couldn't you stop?" Eric asked as he emerged from his office and started down the stairs.

"Nothing, just girl talk." Hazel said and smiled at Bert.

They locked up the office and put a sign on the window they would be back at two o'clock.

"That's a pretty long lunch hour," Hazel laughed.

"I want to go pick out my new truck after lunch. I thought maybe having you two ladies along to give me advice might help," Eric smiled.

"I will enjoy spending some more of your money," Bertha smiled back at him.

Hazel agreed and they walked down the street toward the restaurant.

Chapter Twenty-five

The three ordered Greek Salad's over Potato Salad and were very satisfied.

Eric brought up the topic of Arthur Plant while they were waiting for their check. Art had come into the restaurant with another young woman on his arm and when he could not be seated right away, he left in a huff. "That man is a piece of work," Eric said.

"He comes in every time he has a new woman but always when he knows we can't seat him right away," the waitress told them. "One of these days, I'm going to fool him and have a table for him. He is so tight; when he does get seated he only orders the cheapest thing on the menu."

"That sounds like him," Bert commented. "Thank you for lunch," she said to Eric. "If I had known you were paying, I'd have ordered something more expensive," she teased.

"Yes, thank you Boss. It was delicious," Hazel agreed.

They left the restaurant and started for the car dealership. "Hank is the guy that we bought ours from," Hazel told Eric. "Maybe we can get him before he leaves for lunch."

The women went into the showroom while Eric parked his Lincoln. When he walked in, they were already talking to Hank.

He was very pleased to see them again and shook Eric's hand vigorously. "We will have to order your truck if you want the same one Mrs. Schlinkenmayer drives. She has all the bells and whistles on hers," He turned and smiled at Bert. "I've been expecting you to come in and trade yours," he said to her. "It is almost two years old."

"Not on you life. It only has twelve thousand miles, so I figure I'll get at least another two years out of it," Bert laughed.

"You tell him Schlick. I wish you would sell it. I wouldn't have to order one," Eric told her. He turned to the salesmen and said, "I hope the new ones are as comfortable as Mrs. Schlinkenmayer's.

"It will be," Hank assured him. "Do you want the moon roof and the third seat in the back? It comes standard on most models but you can reduce the price quite a bit if you can wait for them to make yours."

"Yes, I'd like the moon roof, independent suspension, and no third seat in the rear. I would like a better than average C.D. player and speakers. I would also like the Eddie Boyer series and I want it pinstriped. I will be buying it on the X plan so figure on using that", Eric rattled off to the salesman.

The salesman looked at him and said, "You sound like Mrs. Schlinkenmayer. She knew what she wanted too. Do you also know what it will cost?" he asked.

"I know what it better not cost me," Eric smiled at him. My secretary and her husband bought two of them only a couple months ago."

The salesman smiled and disappeared. He was back in five minutes with the price and the name of a dealership he could pick it up from.

Eric was pleased and told him to have it here by the first of the week. He would give the man a deposit today.

"That won't be necessary Eric," the salesman said. "I'll get all the papers drawn up for Monday and you can come in and sign them. Do you want a decorator plate or have you one from another car?"

"I think I'd like the decorator plate. If it is here by Monday, please put it on my new vehicle," Eric told him.

"I'll see to it", the salesman smiled and shock his hand as he led the three to the door.

The two women walked out to Eric's car and got in. He followed shortly after them and said as he entered behind the wheel, "he seems like a nice enough chap. He asked me if I would like a loaner."

Both women went in to fits of laughter and Eric made them explain what was so funny.

When she reached the office, the phone was ringing off the hook. Hazel walked in first and grabbed the first phone she came across. "Yes we just walked in. For some reason the phones didn't transfer to Eric's cell phone. Just a minute, I'll get him," She said, handing the phone to Eric.

"Hoffermeister here," Eric said into the phone. "Of course, I remember you, Chief Davis. Yes, we have been making some inquiries about an Arthur Plant. Could you hold on a moment, I'd like to transfer this to my office? I can speak more freely there." Eric motioned for Bert to transfer the phone call and hurried up to his office. He picked up the phone and said, "I was checking in the states but to be honest, I didn't think to check in Mexico. Yes sir; that would be great. When will you be coming north? Fine, I'll wait for your call. I would suggest you fly into Saginaw and I will pick you up there. No that 's not necessary. If there is anything we have up here its S.U.V's. It is the only way to travel," he laughed. "I'll be looking forward to it," he said and hung up the phone. He called Hazel and asked her to get the car salesmen on the phone right away. When the salesman answered Eric said, "I will need at least two more S.U.V's as soon as possible. Yes, two days will be sufficient. No! They don't need to be Eddie Bowers; in fact I would rather not have them as Eddie Bowers. I need them in non-descriptive colors. Yes, black and tan would be fine. No! No pin stripes. I don't care if they have the third seat or not. If that is all you can get on short notice, get them with the third seat. Yes, use the X plan on both of them and put them in the company's name," he said and rattled off how he wanted the name to appear on the title. Hanging up his phone, he asked Bertha to come up to his office.

She quickly appeared in his doorway. She knew the man he had been talking to was interested in Arthur also. She walked in and Eric asked her to sit down.

"I thought I would bring you up to date," He told her. "That was a call from an old friend of mine living in Mexico. He saw a wire come across the desk of the L.A. Police Department in California he used to work out of. He was visiting his old station house and called to tell me he has been after Arthur for over fifteen years. Every time he thought he had him, Arthur slipped through his fingers. He knows he's dirty but has never been able to prove it. He has retired now and asked if I could use a good man up here. Of course I was happy to hear he might want to work with us, but I think it might be because Art has a sister Lizzie living here somewhere."

"Lizzie Plant; but that can't be, but there couldn't be two Lizzie Plants in this small town," Bert said with a puzzled look on her face. "I never put the two together but it could be possible. They came about the same time and she is about the same age as Art. No! I can't believe they are related. Lizzie is one of the nicest, most helpful women in Michaywe'. She is a nurse at the hospital and whenever someone is ill in Michaywe' she calls to see if she can be of assistance. I've never heard anyone say she has a brother."

"Well Kurt must know something we don't. He will be coming up next month, as soon as he can get everything arranged. He lost his wife last year and has been kind of drifting around, trying to find somewhere to land; I know the feeling, He said. "He will be a big asset to the firm. It solves one problem I have been neglecting."

"What is that?" Bertha asked. She really wanted him to tell her more about Arthur but she knew he would tell it in his own way.

"I need an operative that can move around in a strange place and kind of melt into the woodwork. Kurt is that kind of guy. He makes friends easily and moves around in all walks of life. I've seen him with the elite of L.A. one month and in the disguise of a drug addict, the next. He is phenomenal. I can't wait to see him again. I'll put him up at my place until he gets settled. I should be in my house by the time he gets here. He wants to get something on Arthur in the worst way. He would probably work for nothing, but I'd want him on the payroll as soon as he arrives."

"He is more than welcome at my place if you aren't in yours," Bertha told him and waited patiently for Eric to tell her more.

"Thank you; I don't know just when he is coming. As far as I am concerned the sooner the better. I haven't told you what we found out through our California office." He continued, "It seems our man Arthur has had a couple wives before. The one disappeared on a cruise and the other one died of what appeared to be another drowning. They think he might have helped her along but nothing was ever proven."

"What about the one that disappeared?" Bert asked.

"Arthur, his wife and his sister were on vacation on a large cruise ship, and they said she must have fallen overboard," Eric said. "Each wife was quite wealthy and left him with a ton of money. From what I've been told, he doesn't have to work for the rest of his life."

"How convenient for him," Bertha said. "I wonder where he worked when he lived here." Bert questioned.

"I don't find where he did. He was up to something when he took those business trips but what it was; we haven't determined yet. I think he might have been chasing around on her."

"You'll find out," Bertha smiled.

He smiled at her confidence in him and said "How about dinner at the club tonight. I've asked Hazel and Carl to join us. He has done a beautiful job on my new files. I know he hasn't charged me enough for them. He said you helped so he is only charging me his regular wages. I've put him on a retainer. We can keep him busy. He would like to start doing some detective work whenever I have time to give him a little training. He has signed up for classes in Traverse City. He will be a real asset. There is so much we need done and he is such a jack of all trades, and by working for us it will also give him time to go to college."

"I'll be glad to join you. I could use another meal like a sore tooth but I will enjoy the company," Bertha told him. "I keep thinking about Arthur. I can use something to take my mind off the stinker."

Eric smiled, "Lets you and I call it a day and go buy some Christmas presents for my family."

"You mean you haven't even started your shopping yet?" Bert laughed.

"No, I've been waiting for your help," Eric smiled that wonderful smile of his again and she knew she would help him do anything he asked.

They left telling Hazel to lock up after them. Eric didn't want her there alone and Carl was not expected back for at least an hour. He was out Christmas shopping for Hazel. Carl told his wife he was running errands for Eric.

Chapter Twenty-six

It was obvious they were not going to get all of Eric's shopping done in Gaylord. He had some definite items he was looking for and Bertha suggested they take a trip to Frankenmuth. If he was looking for something special in tree decorations, that was the place to go. They could drive down, shop and be back before nightfall. At dinner when they told Carl and Hazel their plans; they had two more people in the car the next day.

Eric was like a little kid in a candy store. He bought a tree that was already decorated and then added outside lights to his list along with a beautiful Santa clause for his front porch. "What if you don't get in by Christmas?" Bert teased.

"Then I'll put them up in my apartment," he laughed. "In the mean time I'll do the front of your house. I used to be quite a decorator over the holidays in California. People came from all over to look at my displays," he said proudly.

Hazel and Carl had to agree. "Some years I think he over did it a little." Hazel smiled.

"You never told me that," Eric insisted.

"I didn't want to spoil your fun," She laughed.

Bert was going to have a beautiful decorated home if he did all he planned. She tried to stop him, but he purchased doubles of everything. "It will be an early Christmas present for my landlord," he smiled.

"I didn't realize it was this much fun spending someone else's money. I don't know what I'll do when I have to start spending my own again," Bertha laughed.

They were all laughing as they exited the Christmas store and ran smack into Art. "Well so nice to see you having a good time," he commented. "Who's the man that can make you laugh again?" he asked.

"Just a friend. I have lots of friends up here," Bert said and walked on by him.

"Do they all spend the night?" He questioned. "I hope this means you will be staying for a while this time," Art commented.

Eric started to say something to him but Bertha looked at him, pleading him not to say anything to Art.

"It looks like I might," she said and took Eric's arm and headed for the car. "How did he get down here? I sometimes think he is following me."

Eric opened the door for her, saying nothing until he got behind the wheel. Carl and Hazel piled into the backseat after putting all the packages in the back cargo space. He was going to have to be more careful of Schlick. Art had definitely followed them.

"He really gets to you, doesn't he? He won't bother you as long as I'm around, hon. Try to relax. You're tight as a drum. We were having such a good time; don't let him spoil it."

"Your right, I'm sorry. He won't dare call me if he sees your car in the drive. I have been screening all my calls lately but the past couple weeks he has stopped calling. I hope it stays that way."

"If he starts up again, let me answer it a few times and maybe he will get the hint," Eric said. "Now, let's go home and put some of these lights up. We'll have a little eggnog I bought, and get to work," he smiled.

He drove Hazel and Carl to their home and took a rain check on stopping in their place for a cup of coffee.

Eric and Bertha did not talk about Art for the rest of the evening. Bert made them a quick dinner of potato soup she had made the previous day, and homemade bread, while Eric put up several strings of lights around her Blue Spruce trees in the front yard.

Eric told her dinner was better than any old restaurant. Later they sat by the fire and enjoyed a cappuccino, while watching a silly movie about a cat that talked to a dog and solved mysteries.

Around nine, Eric excused himself and went downstairs. It had been one of the most pleasant evenings Bertha had spent in a long time. She went to her room, got into bed and was quickly asleep.

Chapter Twenty-seven

The next day was Sunday so Bert and Eric got up and went to church together. They had a small bowl of fruit before leaving. When the service was over, they joined their friends in the fellowship hall for coffee. Again, they all went to the club for lunch and as soon as Bert and Eric returned home, he got busy on the outside decorations. Bertha laughed, my light bill is going to be a dandy this month, she said to herself, but she really did not care. Everything was so beautiful and the decorations helped her get into the Christmas spirit.

The trees surrounding the circular drive were covered with lights and in the inside of the circle; he had put her Nativity Scene and the Crèche he had purchased for her to go with her Nativity. It had taken up most of the room in the truck and they had to place the other packages tucked around it. She had always meant to buy a Crèche and now she had one to set off her Nativity Scene. He came inside long enough to put the Christ child in the front hall until Christmas Eve. He went back out and hung lights around the garage and along the front porch. After he hung the lights silhouetting the front door, she walked outside with a cup of coffee to warm him. "Don't you think you have enough lights now?" she asked him.

"I have to put out Rudolph with the lighted nose yet, and then I'll quit," He smiled that smile again. The snow had been falling most of the day and was really piling up.

He was having so much fun, she did not want to tell him; enough was enough. Looking at him enjoying his task, hanging lights everywhere, you would not have believed he was the owner of so many detective agencies.

"Come on I'll take you to dinner," Bertha told him. He was starting the snowblower. She smiled and went back inside the house. Her late husband Jeff also insisted he had to plow before they drove on the drive after a heavy snowfall. Bert went into her room and changed into a heavy sweater and slacks. She always felt colder when she could see the snow. In all reality, it was usually warmer when it snowed but her body never believed it. She was finishing her make-up when she heard Eric come in through the garage door.

"I'll only be a few minutes," he yelled to her. "I want to go down and get out of these wet clothes. Will a sweater and slacks be okay to wear to dinner?" he asked.

"Sure, that's what I'm wearing," she answered through her closed bedroom door.

"I'll come up when I'm presentable," he told her.

"Don't be silly. You can come in through the house. That snow must be three feet high," She said as she opened her bedroom door.

He laughed, "No it isn't. I blew out a nice wide path to the back door. That's what took me so long. I'll see you in a few minutes." He went back out, closed the garage door and started around the house, using his new path.

Bertha looked at the clock. It had been an hour since he said he would be in. She was so busy wrapping gifts she had not noticed the time.

Chapter Twenty-nine

Entering the club, they were greeted by a new hostess seated at the desk. "Do you have reservations?" she asked.

Michelle heard them enter and walked out to the reservation desk. "Mrs. Schlinkenmayer was expected," she said. "I'll show them to table six." She led Eric and Bertha to a nice table by a window. She motioned for Bertha's favorite waitress to come over to their table. Bertha smiled at Michelle and thanked her.

"Maybe we are spending too much time here", Eric smiled at Bert as the waitress walked over. He ordered a nice wine and asked to take a few more minutes deciding what to order. We should have the menu memorized by now, but I'm not in any hurry to finish dinner," he said.

Bert looked at him with a question on her face. "That phone call I received, just before we left, was from my old friend, Kurt Davis. He tied up all his loose ends down there and wanted to know if it would be all right to come right away. I couldn't tell him fast enough I would be happy to see him. He will be flying in tonight and I thought, maybe you would ride to Saginaw with me to pick him up. He was calling from Detroit so by the time we eat and drive over there; he should be just getting off the plane."

"I'd love to go with you. I am anxious to hear what he has to say about our friend Art. She had just gotten Art's name out of her mouth when she heard him out at the desk, demanding to be seated immediately.

Michelle knew Bert had been trying to avoid him. She over heard Bert telling Eric that, the day Art went over to her table. It was obvious to Michelle, Bertha could not stand the man and he was hounding her. Michelle said she could seat him in the bar, but there was at least an hour wait for the dining room. She was so sorry; they were a little short of help. Of course, Art would have none of that and huffed out of the club with his latest young girl on his arm. Michelle came into the dining room and smiled at Bertha as she passed their table. "And you thought we spend too much time here. She knew we didn't want him coming to our table and he would have, if he had known we were here," Bert said.

"He is a real piece of work; but I guess I've said that before. I would like to call him a name I think really fits him, but there is a lady present," he said. "Let's order, I'm hungry."

They ordered the special and they both agreed the Salmon was prepared to perfection. "There is just enough dill to make it tasty," Bert said

.   "I was trying to place the taste. Dill huh! I'll have to remember that. I hope you and Kurt don't mind the smell of garlic," he laughed, "but I'm not going to forfeit eating these red potatoes and they are laced with it."

"I feel the same. We can have a mint when we get there and maybe it won't be too bad," Bertha laughed. "I hope Kurt will be comfortable in your spare room, until he finds a place. We can all celebrate Christmas together."

"That's very nice of you Schlick," he said.

"He hasn't any family and probably wanted to come now instead of spending the Holidays alone," Bertha stated

. "I'm sure you will like him. Just don't like him too much. He is a good looking guy," he smiled.

They finished their meals and left the club, heading for Saginaw. They thought they would arrive in plenty of time before Kurt's plane arrived, but when they looked at the arrival board, they discovered the plane had been in for fifteen minutes. Eric went to the baggage area on the run, and asked Bert to watch the outside door leading to the parking lot.

A voice behind her said, "Hello Mrs. Schlinkenmayer."

Bertha turned to find a dark handsome man with a beautiful mustache, looking down on her. "Yes," she said. "You must be Kurt. Please call me Bert. How did you know it was me?" she asked.

"Oh! I'd know you anywhere. Eric gave me a great description of you, but I must tell you I thought he had exaggerated, but I see he didn't," he smiled.

"Some day I'm going to ask him what that description is. He's used it several times. His secretary knew me too," she smiled. "Oh! Here comes the man now."

Eric walked up and gave his friend a big bear hug. "Man! You look terrific. You haven't changed a day," Eric told him.

"You have old friend. You have much better taste in women," Kurt smiled.

Bertha did not say anything. She did not know how much Eric had told his friend of their relationship. She wasn't sure she wanted to know; or did she? They went out and got into Bert's car. Eric and Kurt sat in the front and Bertha rode in the back seat. She insisted she sit in back so the two men could talk. Kurt said it would be nice to be chauffeured so he could watch the scenery to see if he could tell why Eric would ever leave California. He looked into the backseat and winked at her. Bertha laughed a nervous laugh and thought to herself, it was so dark the man could not see anything if he wanted too.

Eric and Kurt talked all the way home. Bertha learned more about Eric than she had learned in all the time she'd known him. From what Kurt said, Eric was very highly thought of in the investigative field.

"He would never tell you," Kurt told Bert, "but he solved several cases with me and one I had been working on for over a year. He seems to have a nose for sniffing out lost clues. I'm hoping between the two of us we can nail Old Plant."

"I sure hope you will. He is really an evil person," Bert told him. "He was married to a friend of mine and was always knocking her around when she was alive."

"That's our Plant. Is she one that supposedly committed suicide?" He asked Eric.

"Yes; we think that was his latest victim," Eric said. "Tomorrow we will go to the office and I'll fill you in on what we have so far."

"Sounds good to me; the sooner the better. Did you find me a place to stay?" He asked.

"Only the best in town; you will be staying with me until you decide whether you plan on stay around a while. I'm staying at Bertha's in her lower level, until my house is completed," Eric told him.

Kurt was not sure he wanted to stay in the lower level of a house. It sounded too much like a basement to him, but he would manage for one night. He could find a place the next day. However, he was pleasantly surprised when Eric showed him Bert's lovely lower level.

"This is sure great compared to that first place you had me spend the night," Kurt teased his friend. "This is one of your better places to rest up."

Eric laughed, "That place sure was awful wasn't it. You have to admit, my new house wasn't bad," he said.

Bertha enjoyed listening to the two men banter back and forth.

"Yeah! The last one was okay," Kurt told him.

"Well folks if you'll excuse me, I'm going to unpack, take a long shower and flop for the night," Kurt told them.

"I'll come down later. I want to talk to Bert for a few minutes," Eric told Kurt.

Bertha fixed them both a cup of coffee. "I wanted to talk to you before we go to the office in the morning," he told Bert. She smiled and waited for him to continue. "I will be in and out of the office quite a bit for the next week," he continued. "Kurt and I have a lot of information to exchange and a lot of territory to cover, and I'd like to get it done by the end of next week. I want our Holiday's free. I thought we might show him some of this great state and convince Kurt to stay even after we solve Nancy's mystery."

"I'll do what I can to help, you know that," Bert told him.

"I just don't want you thinking I'm neglecting you," Eric told her. He moved over and sat on the ottoman at the foot of her chair.

"Don't give it another thought. We will have the Holiday's together and I don't expect to monopolize your time," Bertha told him.

"You could never do that. I enjoy every minute we are together. I think you know that," Eric said, taking her hand. "I've tried not to be too obvious about how I feel about you, as long as I'm under your roof, but I think you know I'm very much in love with you."

Bert did not know what to say. She finally got her voice and said, "You haven't known me very long. How can you be so sure?" she asked.

"I knew it when I saw you on the stage in Branson. I've been looking for you for a lot of years," he smiled. "There is something else you should know."

"What is that?" she asked unable to say more.

"It was not a coincidence I was at that camp ground. I had been following you for several weeks," he said. Bertha looked up in shock. "No! It's nothing like that. Let me explain." He took a deep breath and continued. "It's about you and Max. I have known Max since we were both small children. We grew up together."

This really surprised Bertha and she said, "My Max?"

"Yes dear. He hired me to keep an eye on you until you got to Michigan."

"Was Elizabeth in on the charade?" Bert asked.

"No! The first time I met her was when you introduced me to her the night we went to dinner. I didn't want you to know about this until I had time to explain Schlick. I am so nuts about you; I don't want any secrets between us. Max meant well. He had no idea I would fall so hard for you. When I told him he said you would be a hard sell and he was right." There went that smile again. "I don't blame you if you're upset, but honey I just laid my heart at your feet and hope you don't stomp on it." He sat back waiting for her to say something.

Bertha leaned forward, smiled and kissed him on the cheek. "You better go see if your friend needs anything. I have a phone call to make and some thinking to do," she told Eric.

"Don't be sore at Max. It's not his fault he is so crazy about his mother-in-law and he wanted to protect her. He described you to me and I thought he was nuts until I met you," he smiled again.

"Sometime I want you to tell me how he described me to you," she smiled. "Though now I would like some time to myself. You have dumped a lot on me all of a sudden and it will take me a little time to digest it all," she said and got up from her seat.

Eric stood and took her in his arms; she did not resist. He kissed her tenderly on her lips and she responded more than she thought possible.

Releasing her he said, "Remember I love you and I won't do this again until I get into my own place. Then I don't guarantee a thing." He smiled and she knew his meaning.

"I hope your house gets done in a hurry. I wouldn't want to wait too long on the next kiss," she said and turned, picking up their cups and took them to the kitchen.

He smiled at her departing back and left returning to the lower level and his room.

Bertha walked over to the phone and called her son-in-law. When Elizabeth answered, she talked to her for a few minutes and then Bertha asked to speak to Max.

"He is right here. Is anything wrong, are you okay?" she anxiously questioned.

"No dear, nothings wrong. I couldn't be better. I only want to talk to Max for a moment," Bert said. Max came to the phone and Bertha said, "I don't know if I should smack you or thank you."

"He told you," he said and Bertha heard her daughter in the back ground say "who told her what?" He ignored his wife and continued. "Mom I just wanted to see you arrived safely."

"Yes dear, I know but did you have to pick such a good looking guy?" she teased.

Max laughed and she heard her daughter say, "WHAT did WHO tell my mother?"

Max turned to his wife and said, "I'll tell you in a minute. Let me finish my conversation with Your Mother."

Elizabeth turned, went into the next room and picked up the phone. She lifted it up very gently in time to hear her mother say, "He said he has been in love with me since Branson."

"How do you feel about it Mom?" Max asked.

"I'm not sure, but I know I feel very strongly about him," She hesitated and added, "Yes, I think I'm in love with him," Bert said.

Elizabeth could not hold back, "MOTHER," she yelled into the phone. "Daddy has been gone less than two years. How could you get involved with a man so quickly and who is he. Is he a professional?"

"Elizabeth, you sound like a snob. Yes, he is a professional. He owns and operates several detective agencies," Bert told her daughter.

"Oh Lord, Mother! You're talking about that Eric fellow. He is younger then you are. WHAT can you be thinking? I knew we should have made you stay with us," Elizabeth told her mother. "I don't know where your head is; and he's living in your home."

Max cut into the conversation. "Elizabeth, he is closer to Bertha's age than you are to mine, and he and I have known each other since childhood. He comes from as a good a family as either one of us. His dad was a doctor and his mother a professor at the university. Now please get off the phone; I'll talk to you later."

Elizabeth knew by the tone of his voice that she should back off, so she hung up.

"I'm sorry Max. I think you are going to be in for it. I didn't want to tell her anything until I could see her at Christmas. She doesn't have to worry about Eric. We have agreed not to go any farther with our relationship until he moves into his own place," Bertha told him.

"Don't worry about it dear. She knows her mother is a lady of morals, and Eric is not that kind of guy; he is and always will be a gentleman," Max assured her.

"I know dear. Now, we better get off the phone so you can go soothe your wife. Tell her I am happy for the first time since her father's death. Maybe that will help. You can also tell her there was no way she could have made me move anywhere I didn't want too," She said this with a smile in her voice.

Max laughed, "I told her that before. I'll take care of it, Mom. I am so happy for you both. I didn't plan it this way but I am pleased. Two of my favorite people may get together. We'll see you right after Christmas. Enjoy yourself Mom. You deserve it. I know Jeff would be pleased," Max told her, hanging up the phone and went in to set his wife straight in her thinking.

Bertha got off the phone and went in to change for bed. She looked in the mirror and said out loud "I'm glad that is over with. Maybe by the time they get up here Elizabeth will have a change of heart and treat Eric properly," but she was not sure her daughter would come around that quickly. She dressed into her nightwear and crawled beneath the sheet. She fell asleep thinking about how long it would be before Eric would kiss her again. She had a smile on her face as she nodded off.

Chapter Thirty

The next morning Elizabeth rang her Mother. "Hi Mom, please don't interrupt until I am through," she told Bertha.

Bert steeled her-self for what she was afraid her daughter was about to say. "Alright dear, I'm listening," she answered.

"Mom, first I want to say I was really off base last night. As attractive and young as you are, you shouldn't stay single forever. I know dad would want you to be happy and he always said you were the best wife and mother he knew. It is only natural you would want to continue being a wife; you're so good at it. I hope, some day I am half as good. I just want to apologize for my outburst. You have every right to like whom you want even to love someone if you want too. Max tells me Eric is one in a million and you know we think you are one in a million, so it is only natural you two should get together. That's all I have to say, except I really apologize," her daughter told her. They were both crying before Elizabeth finished her little speech.

"Thank you dear. I know you really want me to be happy and right now, I am. It may not come to anything but at least I know I won't lose my daughter if I get together with Eric. You will really like him, dear. He is a very nice person," Bert told her.

"Mom, you wouldn't get mixed up with any other kind. Good luck! If you want him, go get him," she laughed.

Bert laughed back. "I may not be able to do anything about it. He's an awfully good looking guy and the women all give him the once over," she said.

"Mom, look in the mirror. He would be lucky to get you," Elizabeth said.

"Well honey, I've got to go. I told them I would hold the office open today. Kurt, the new detective working for Eric is going to be briefed on the agency and will be busy all day with Eric and his secretary, getting caught up. They need someone on the phones. Thanks again for calling, honey. I needed to hear from you. You're the best daughter anyone could ask for."

"Thanks, Mom, but sometimes I don't sound like one. I am just thankful you're so forgiving. See you soon," she told her mother and hung up the phone.

Max, she said to herself, I don't know what you said or did, but thank you. Bert went out to the car and headed for the office.

Chapter Thirty-one

Bertha arrived at the office before anyone else. She unlocked the door and the phone was ringing off the hook. She walked over to the phone and answered, "Hoffermeister Confidential Services; May I help you."

"You can come over to the restaurant and have breakfast with us. I would have asked you in person but I heard you on the phone before I left this morning so I thought I'd call after we got here. Kurt is a bear before he has his coffee. Will you join us?" Eric asked.

Bertha knew where he was and she had not taken time for breakfast so she told them she would be there in about five minutes. She put the phones back on the answering machine and locked the door behind her. She did not bother going to her car. She walked up the street to the restaurant and entered to find Eric, Kurt and Hazel seated in a booth. She walked over and took the seat next to Hazel. "Hello, have you ordered?" she asked.

"No we were waiting for you," Eric smiled that smile again.

Bertha automatically smiled back at him and felt the warmth go through her. She hoped her face was not red and last night was not written on it. She managed to order and when everyone started talking, she began to relax and enjoy the morning. She was having her last cup of coffee when Eric and Kurt excused themselves and went up to the cashier to pay their bill.

"Let me get this," she heard Kurt say. "This is the least I can do. You people have made it so easy for me to adjust to my new surroundings. I think I will really enjoy it here. Did you ask Bert to look for a house for me to rent?" he asked while they were waiting for change.

"No, I figured we had plenty of time for that," Eric said.

"We do, but I don't know how long it will be before we nail this guy and I would like to be in my own place. I don't want my wanderlust to take over. If I sign a lease, I can't very well move," Kurt smiled and Eric had to agree with him. Eric knew his pal moved around a lot after he lost his wife. He went back over to Bert and asked her to look for a place for Kurt as soon as possible. He told her about Kurt's moving every month or so and wanted to get him tied down for six months to a year.

"I think I can get him a place fairly quick. He may need to buy a little furniture, because the place I have in mind is in Michaywe'. It belongs to a friend of mine. He is looking for a good renter and will give an option to buy the place," Bert told him.

"Sounds good. Why don't you get in contact with your friend and find out what kind of deal you can get and then go see what Kurt will need to purchase to finish furnishing the place. He will need very little probably, just the necessities. He doesn't stay home much. See you later and Thank you very much, Mrs. Schlinkenmayer," Eric reached for her hand, giving it a warm squeeze.

She smiled up at him and he left to join Kurt outside. Hazel smiled at her and said, "I think my boss has a thing for you. I hope it is mutual. He is a great guy and needs someone in his life."

"You old married people are always looking to get your single friends hooked up with someone," Bert laughed. "Come on matchmaker, we've got work to do," she told her and got up to leave.

Art walked up behind her and said, "Well if it isn't Miss Morals. You don't want anything to do with me but your new boyfriend sleeps over."

"He is my boss and is renting the lower level from me until his house gets built. If that is any business of yours," Bertha angrily bit back at him. "And how do you know he stays at night; are you a stalker as well as a wife beater?" She knew as soon as she said it, she had said too much. Art's face got red and before he could do or say anything; Eric was back.

"Excuse me Art," Eric said, "but I have to tell Mrs. Schlinkenmayer something." Art backed off and left the restaurant.

"Bert, don't even talk to that man. I'm glad we saw him walk over to your table after we left. I watched him looking us over while we had breakfast. He was setting two booths behind us. We were watching through the window just in case. He couldn't wait to get to you. He really worries me. What did he say?" Eric asked.

Bertha voiced their conversation and Hazel added, "Bertha put him in his place but he was furious. I thought he was going to hit her."

"Just stay away from him, if possible. He is dangerous. I'm sure of it. I'll need a lift back to the office. Kurt took the car so he can tail Art. I had the extra car delivered to the parking space behind our building and will join Kurt on the stake out. We both have safe cell phones and can communicate without worrying about someone picking up our calls.

They left the restaurant together and rode in Hazel's car. They dropped Eric off behind the building and then drove back to park in front of the office.

Hazel unlocked the door and they walked inside. Bert found several messages for Eric and gave them to Hazel. Next she called her friend in Michaywe' and talked to him about his rental. He was pleased Bertha would vouch for Kurt and told her where to find the key. She and Hazel would check it out during their lunch hour. The morning flew by and before she knew it, Hazel was at her side suggesting they go to lunch. Bert smiled and put the phones back on the answer machine. They left the building and went over to check out the house before they went to the restaurant.

Chapter Thirty-two

It was a nice home on a beautiful lot, with a garage big enough to keep Kurt's S.U.V and leave room for the portable lab he always carried with him. The only furnishings he might need would be a bedroom suite, a couple recliners and a T.V. Bert had enough dishes, pots and pans and flatware to keep him happy and she would donate them to Kurt's new home. When they had breakfast, Kurt mentioned that he did not cook and was seldom home for meals. The recliners and TV's were for him and Eric to watch football games. Their next stop was the local furniture stores. They looked at several bedroom suites and then left for lunch. During their lunch, Bert called down state on her cell phone to her grandpa's old furniture store. The gentleman that answered the phone was just the person she wanted to talk too. He and his parents, who were both long gone, had purchased the store from Bert's family estate many years ago, after she lost both her grandparents and parents the same year. He now ran it alone with the help of four employees. He still gave Bert a huge discount. She asked about the leather recliners she had purchased the year before and he said she could still get them at the same cost. Kurt had admired them the first time he saw them and immediately went over and tried one on for size. He said he wanted two when he was settled into his own place. She ordered four of them and had them shipped up state. She knew Eric would be pleased she ordered his also. He had mentioned it several times but she had not gotten around to it before.

That settled, Bert tackled the Greek Salad and devoured it completely. Usually she only ate half and took the other half home for the next day but today she had worked up an enormous appetite. "Spending money always makes me hungry," she gave as an explanation to Hazel. Hazel laughed and told her it usually worked the opposite with her but today, since they were spending someone else's money, she also had a good appetite.

They finished their lunches and headed back to the office. When they entered, they found Eric waiting for them.

"You've been at the furniture store, the restaurant and just returned to the office," he said. It was not a question; it was a fact.

"How do you know where we've been?" Bertha asked him.

"We have been following Art, and he has been following you," Eric told her.

"O Lord! What can we do about it? He really gives me the creeps. You're going to be moving after the first of the year. What will I do then?" Bert said.

"Don't worry about it. Chief Hanraty went to the courthouse and is bringing a Cease and Desist order to present to our friend Art. Kurt went and talked to Hanraty as soon as we were sure he was going to keep stalking you. He won't be able to get within a hundred yards of you," Eric smiled and added, "I won't be moving to my new house until I know Art is behind bars and you're safe." He walked over and put his arms around Bert and she leaned her head on his shoulder. She had been shaking like a leaf and it helped having him so near. She did not think how it might look to Hazel and she did not care. She need not have worried. Hazel was behind her and smiling at her boss.

Twenty minutes later the orders arrived and Bertha signed them. The chief walked out to Art's car and said, "Arthur Plant this is for you." He handed the papers to a very surprised Art. "It is an order to stay away from Mrs. Schlinkenmayer, and if you get within one hundred yards of her or call her on the phone, you will be arrested. Is that clear?" He did not wait for an answer, but added, "If that happens; I for one will see you get the maximum sentence the law allows. Now get out of here." He walked back inside the building as Art was pulling away. "That should take care of him for a while. I almost hope he doesn't stop. I'd love to get his butt in my jail," the chief smiled.

"Thanks chief. I have to be out of town for a few days and I would appreciate it if you would kind of keep track of Mrs. Schlinkenmayer's here and at her home. Just until we are sure that toad is going to obey the law," Eric told him.

"Be happy too. Maybe you could have dinner with my wife and me tonight," the chief said, with a smile.

"Thank you for the invitation but I have to be at chorus tonight at seven," Bert told him.

"We could have an early dinner. My wife has to be at a chorus meeting too. We will come by and pick you up, have dinner and then I will take you both to your practice. When I take you home, I can check the house and grounds," He told Bert.

"That's not necessary," Bert said. "I don't want to put you out."

"Let the chief help, Bert. I'll be home tomorrow and I'll worry a lot less," Eric said.

Bert smiled at him and said, "Okay, worry wart, but I think we have seen the last of Art for a while. He thinks you're staying at my place and he has always been a coward. He won't try to get into my home when he thinks he may run into a man."

"I'll leave my car there and we'll use Kurt's. Then he won't know we are out of town," Eric assured her. Eric and Kurt left shortly after the chief and Bertha went back to work. Hazel went to her office. Bert noted Hazel left her door open. She was not going to take any chances someone would come in and bother Bert. Hazel had so much to do she finally called Bert and asked her to come up and help her with some filing. Bert did not have the heart to tell her she disliked filing almost as much as a trip to the dentist but she went up and spent the remainder of the day, doing little jobs; trying to give Hazel whatever help she could with any of Hazel's minor chores. They did take time to have a snack brought in and ate at Hazel's desk.

Bert left when Hazel left and she headed home. She was excited to see Eric's car in the drive until she remembered he was not going to be there. She went in and turned her security system on "stay." She would leave it on all the time for a while. Normally she only turned it on when she left the house. At five, she was ready and waiting for the Chief and his wife Ann.

When they arrived she quickly turned off the system and the chief came in to check the doors and windows. "You've met my wife Ann," he said to Bert as they walked through the door.

"Ann! My goodness I didn't realize you're the chief's wife. I guess I've been away too long. I don't know half the new gals in the chorus. I will have to pay more attention to names. I have been trying to concentrate on the notes and words to all the new songs," Bertha tried to explain.

"I don't publicize the fact Gary is a cop. It intimidates some people. There are probably a lot of the women that don't know yet what my husband does for a living," Ann graciously told Bert.

"Okay ladies, let's get going. I want to have enough time to eat without rushing through the meal," Gary told them. "And please call me Gary, Bertha. Chief is for the people I work with. All my friends call me Gary."

"Thank you Gary," Bert said, "I much prefer first names. With a moniker like Schlinkenmayer, most people prefer Bert.

They left and went to the club.   Gary wanted to check it out first and went inside the dining room. He wanted to be sure Art was not there. He was not, so he went out and escorted the two women into the building. The hostess walked over and asked, "You have more company?"

"No! They live in Gaylord and are my guests tonight," Bert said. After they were seated she told them about the once over the little hostess always gave Eric. "He thinks she is harmless; I'm not so sure," Bert laughed.

"If she looked at my man the way she does yours; I'd be a little leery too," Ann smiled.

Bert did not correct the 'my man' reference. I guess Eric was Bert's man. She smiled at Ann and both women knew what the other was thinking.

They took their time eating and later Gary took them to the church, where they rehearsed. When they walked in together, the women were already doing their warm-up exercises.

Chief Hanraty was waiting for them after their practice and they climbed back into his squad car. They went directly to Bert's home and before she entered, he checked all the doors, windows and security system before he left and then took his wife home.

Annette called her as soon as the police car left Bert's drive. "Is everything okay over there?" she asked anxiously. "I saw the police car.

"Yes! I was out to dinner with the new chief of police. He wanted to check my home before he left. Eric will be gone for a couple days and I had to get a restraining order out against Art. He has been stalking me," Bertha told her.

"I'm coming over," She said. "I'll bring my things. I'm going to stay the night. I wouldn't trust that guy to stay away just because there is a little restraining order out against him," Annette told her over Bertha's protests, five minutes later she was at her door. She had driven and left her car in the driveway in plain sight.

Bert greeted her friend at the door and thanked her for coming. "It really isn't necessary but I will feel better having someone else here." Bert told her. Bertha went back in and turned the alarm back on and then showed Annette to her guestroom. She had bi-passed the upstairs motion detector as she always did whenever she had guests stay over night.

They talked for a few minutes and Annette said, "You better get to bed. You've had a long day."

Bert had to admit she was very tired. She thanked Annette again for coming and went in to change for the night. Bert felt very secure and quickly fell asleep.

Around midnight Annette came into Bert's room. "Shhhh," she said putting her finger to her lips. I think that stinker is up on the back deck. I wish we could turn the lights on out there."

"We can. I have the master switch here in my room," she said and walked over and switched on the lights. Chief Hanraty appeared in the window. Bert went over and opened the door a crack. "What is it?" she asked.

"Nothing Bert, I thought I saw someone on your deck so I came up to investigate," He said through the partially open door. "Everything is fine. Go back to bed."

"Have you been out there all evening?" she asked him.

"Yes, Ann and I thought we would hang around for a little while," he smiled at her.

"Well don't stay out there any longer. You either come in or go home. As you see I have someone staying with me and I'm sure we will be fine," Bert told him.

"Okay, but you call me if you hear anything," he said and gave her his card; writing his home phone number on the back. "I'll see you in the morning," he added in parting.

"I'm to be at the office early," Bert told him. "Why don't you stop in for coffee about nine thirty? I'll bring in some rolls," she smiled.

"Sounds good to me; see you then," he said and left, walking back to his car where he had parked it on the street behind her home. He had a flashlight or he never would have made it through the brush and trees. He had to walk almost a quarter of an acre in the dark.

Bert smiled, "He parked so he could watch both side yards and the back yard. He knows what he is doing; that's for sure. I'm sorry he had to spend so much of his evening watching my house. I feel guilty sleeping through his stake-out."

"Don't, he was doing what he wanted to do. Now let's try to get back to sleep," Annette told her, and left for the guestroom.

To Bert's surprise, she immediately fell asleep again.

Chapter Thirty-three

Bertha arrived at the office and went up to see Hazel. She found her already busy typing up reports. "Good morning," she said. "Chief Hanraty is going to be here in the next half hour and I promised him coffee and a roll. I picked some up at the bakery before I came in. Would you like to join us for a roll with your coffee?" Bert asked her.

"No thanks, just coffee; when you have time," Hazel told her. "Maybe, when Carl gets here; he wants to stick pretty close until Eric gets back. I know Carl will eat your rolls," she smiled up at Bert. When Bert left the room, Hazel got right back to typing at her computer. When she got most of her work caught up, she was going to go downstairs and join them before the guys ate up all the rolls.

Bert had just finished making the coffee when the Chief walked in. "Am I too early?" he asked.

"No not at all. We've been here for almost an hour. Carl will be joining us shortly. He is as bad as you are; he won't let us out of his sight either," she smiled at the Chief.

"Oh, I think our boy has got the news. I don't think he will bother you until he thinks we have forgotten about him," Gary told her.

"Here comes Carl now. I don't think you two have met one another," she said and made the introductions. "Carl is Eric's right hand man and his wife Hazel is his private secretary. They moved from California to help Eric get his new office established."

The Chief and Carl started talking and when Hazel took time to join them for coffee and rolls, they did not stop. "I see Carl and Gary have met," Hazel smiled.

"Oh, I am sorry. I think you've met my wife, chief," Carl said.

"Yes! Good morning Hazel," the chief said and got up to give her a chair.

Gary smiled and told her how pleased they were to have them both join the community. After coffee and a couple of rolls, he excused himself by saying, "I better get to work. I haven't checked into the office today and I know there will be a pile of work on my desk." He left and Carl and Hazel talked while Bert went back to answering the phones.

Around noon, Eric walked into the office. He had a full day's growth of beard on his face and she hardly recognized him. He said, "Let me go up and get presentable before we talk," and started up the stairs.

"I'm sorry sir, but that is my boss's private offices and no bums are allowed," Bert teased.

"If you don't behave, I'll come back down there and give you a big whisker burn before I clean up.   That will quiet you down," He threatened, but proceeded up the stairs.   Ten minutes later, her handsome boss came back down, wearing a suit, shirt and tie.   He had shaved and removed the beard.   "How about some lunch love," he grinned that grin.

"Love too, if you're sure my boss won't mind," Bert said, and got up from her chair and came around the desk. "I'll ask Hazel to man the phones until we get back."

"Already taken care of, my dear. I told her we would manage the office after we get back; if she and Carl can do without us for a little while," He told her while giving her a hug and a light kiss. "I don't really care if an operator is on the phones one hundred percent of the time until we open in January."

The two walked out into the crisp December air. "It smells so clean here," Eric told her. "I usually don't breathe anything I can't see," he laughed.

"That's an old one," she laughed back, "but it is wonderful breathing clean air. I was never conscious of the air when I lived in California. I guess it was because we lived in Mission Viejo and there was seldom smog. The Santa Ana winds would blow through periodically and throw all sorts of leaves and trash around but that was the extent of bad air.   It didn't take us long to figure out we needed a pool cover."   Bert laughingly told him and held his hand while they walked to the restaurant.

"I would like to do a little more shopping before lunch if you don't mind. I'd want to get

Hazel and Carl some warm gloves and hats," Eric told her.

"They can always use a warm hat and gloves. I know just where to get them too," she told him and steered him into the shop they were approaching.

They found what he wanted. He took two pair of leather gloves; one lined with fur and one dress leather. He also found a fur hat he liked and purchased it as well. "Now let's go across the street to the men's shop and get Carl's. Then I will be finished with my shopping," Eric said.

They went across and found the same two pair of gloves for men. He purchased those, and then found an Envelope Hat, in fur and paid for the hat. "I think I'll get one for me too," he said and told them not to bag one. "I'll wear this one," he told the clerk, placing it on his head as they walked out. They left for lunch promising both shops they would be back in about an hour and pick up their packages. Eric was having them gift-wrapped and Bertha teased him about not wrapping them himself.

"You have never seen the way I wrap a gift," he laughed.

"I can't imagine someone who has the imagination you have decorating at Christmas time, not being able to wrap a boxed gift. I would have helped you. It really isn't that hard once you learn how to wrap the first one," she assured him.

They ate lunch, left the restaurant and picked up their packages. Eric and Bertha walked in to find Carl and Hazel ready to leave. "Do we have time to do a little shopping," Carl asked. "Hey! Nice hat," he said to Eric.

"Thanks, I just bought it. Yes, go ahead and take your time. I won't expect you two back for at least a couple hours," Eric told them. "That will give you time to drive to some of the stores in the township. Oh! I don't want any office equipment," he laughed, "but I could use some linens."

"Who said we were getting you anything," Hazel teased him. "Come on Carl before he gives you a list." Taking Carl's arm, they walked outside and started to go over to their car.

"Be careful of that air," Eric yelled as they opened the door. "It is so clean, it worries me."

Carl and Hazel were laughing outside the building. Bert went to her desk and answered a call. "Hoffermeister's," she said and before she could finish the company's title, the man on the other end said he wanted to talk to Eric, immediately. Bertha motioned for Eric to get the phone and he hurried up to his office as she buzzed the call through to his phone. She was surprised Eric was on the phone for twenty minutes. He never took that long to answer a call. When he hung up, she heard no more from him until Carl and Hazel walked in after their two-hour lunch and shopping spree.

Eric heard them return and called down, "Hazel will you take over the phones, and I'd like Mrs. Schlinkenmayer to come to my office."

Bertha put the call transfer to Hazel's office phone and went up to Eric's office. "Here I am, boss. What do you need?" she asked.

"I'm too busy for what I really need," he smiled at her. "Please have a chair. That phone call was from Kurt. He's at the Chief's office. I think we better take some time for a long talk," He added.

"You sound very serious," she said.

"Yes! Kurt is very upset. Let me go back a little," he said. "First, that trip we took was back to California. We wanted to talk to the inspector in charge of Art's first wife's death. The authorities were assured she had drowned in a boating accident. The officer told us he never had the time to do a complete investigation. He thought it smelled of murder from day one; especially after his second wife died of drowning in the pool, but the then chief of police was Art's buddy and the chief kept pushing the officer to release the body and get on with his other assignments. Later the officer took the file out and put it in his desk wanting to get at it later, when he had more time. He never had the time to do much with it. Now he thinks he can get the case open again and maybe get the body exhumed for a further, complete autopsy. With the new methods in DNA we are hoping he can find further evidence Art murdered her," he told her.

"That sounds wonderful. Not that the poor woman was murdered, but that Art will be exposed as a killer. If he did it once, he might do it again. It would make it a lot easier for us to get Nancy's case reopened. How long before they let us know if they found anything?" Bertha asked.

"Don't be in a hurry. He wants to take it nice and slow and give himself plenty of time to get the body back on the examining table. That is not all I wanted to talk to you about. I won't be moving into my house until we know one way or the other that Art is out of the picture," Eric told her.

"As much as I enjoy the company; do you think that is necessary? I don't think he will bother me anymore," Bertha told him.

"That is where you're wrong, dear. He has stopped following you around but is now following Carl and Hazel. He even had the nerve to approach them at lunch today. Trying to pump them for more information on why you were working when it wasn't necessary and why a detective company. He suggested maybe it was because there was something going on between the two of us," Eric told her.

"The man's smarter than I thought," she smiled at Eric, "but I can see where it would bother you, as it does me; that he is following Carl and Hazel. What did Kurt have to say about that?" Bertha asked.

Eric told her what Kurt told him and hesitated, waiting for her reaction. When she did not say anything, he continued. "He was at police headquarters and they are filing another, Cease and Desist order against Art, demanding he stay away from the office or their home and far away from Carl and Hazel," he told her. "He'll be served as soon as Carl goes over and signs the papers. Kurt has been following him everywhere since he got here and he said he is at his home or was an hour ago."

"Good, he is becoming a real pest," Bert said. "Are we going to dinner tonight?" She asked trying to get her mind off Art.

"Yes, but I have to make a few stops first. Why don't you go home and I'll be along shortly," He suggested. "I wanted you aware of my staying for a while longer. I made a promise and it is becoming too hard for me to keep it." She knew what he meant.

"We are both adults. I think we can handle it. We will stay away from certain rooms and subjects," she smiled.

Bert was glad to get away early. She still had several more things to do. It was just three days before Christmas and she knew she would need more food in the house with all the company she was expecting and if Eric was with her, he might wonder why she was purchasing all the extra food.

Chapter Thirty-four

Eric left the office and was only a half block away, just turning the corner to pick up his car from the parking lot when he felt it. He had been shot in the back. He fell forward against a lamppost and slid to the cold wet sidewalk. He was lucky he hit the lamppost as it aided him as he fell, instead of falling face forward onto the cement. He thought he heard his friend Kurt before he lost consciousness.

He had heard Kurt. He was yelling as he grabbed Art around the neck, twisting his gun arm behind his back, as he was about to shoot Eric the second time. The shot went astray. Kurt was still yelling when he took Art, not too gently to the ground, putting his knee in his back and reaching for his handcuffs simultaneously. He cuffed him and heard Art say, "She deserves better than a cheap detective. I hope I killed him."

"You better pray he isn't dead," he told Art and put a call through on his cell phone to get the E.M.T. from the hospital that was located only minutes away. He still had his knee in Art's back when he felt the fight go out of him. Art was whining as Kurt took him to the lamp post down the block and removed one cuff long enough to put his hands behind his back around the post snapping the lose cuff on Art's free wrist. He let him slide down in a sitting position and went over to his friend. Art was already complaining his arms hurt being tied behind his back, as Kurt went and knelt beside Eric.

He did not touch him but kept calling his name. He thought he saw Eric's eyes flutter and he felt a strong pulse in his pal's neck. The Emergency vehicle arrived and the paramedics took over. When they turned Eric to put him on the stretcher, Kurt saw the spent bullet on the ground. It must have gone all the way through his friend without hitting bone. He told the paramedics not to touch it until the police arrive. He heard the police siren as he was speaking to them.

The police rushed over and Kurt quickly filled them in on the last five minutes. It felt like he was crouched over Eric for an hour and was surprised when he looked at his watch to tell the officer in charge what time the shot was fired.

Two of the officers took Kurt's key and placed Art in their squad car. When they returned his key, Kurt's training took over and he started barking orders as though he was still a chief of police. "Start looking for another bullet. He got off the second shot as I was grabbing him. I think it may be in a post of one of those street signs. He shot as I was pulling his gun behind his back." The officers did not argue. They knew a pro when they heard one and this guy seemed to know what he was doing. Just then, the local Chief of

Police arrived. He stopped the paramedics as they were putting Eric into the ambulance long enough to see Eric was still breathing.

Gary walked over to Kurt and said, "Looks like we pushed him far enough. Too bad Eric was shot. The medics said he would make it but he is headed for the operating room. Have you called Bertha?"

"Not yet. Things have been going so fast. That slime ball tried to get off a second shot, but I got there just in time. I have your men looking for the second bullet but they probably won't have much luck until daylight," Kurt told him.

"Well, I'm here now. You take off and look after your friend. We'll find that bullet if we have to look all night. I have the one from the body that went clear through and will take charge of it. Now, stop worrying. We may be a small town police force, but we're good. The men I brought with me are all former big city cops. They are going to love doing something besides stopping cars for speeding," Gary smiled, trying to get Kurt to calm down. Kurt was wound up like a tight spring ready to break. "You better go to the hospital and I will have one of my men go pick up Bertha."

"Yeah, thanks. Tell your man to only tell her he is at the hospital but is going to be fine. She will panic if she finds out he's been shot in the back," Kurt said.

"Leave it to me," the Chief told him and gave orders to one of the arresting officers standing next to him to take his car and go pick up Mrs. Schlinkenmayer from her home and bring her to the hospital. He went back to his detectives and started talking to them.

The chief called his wife and asked her to go to the hospital as soon as possible. He filed her in on the evening's events. He would meet her there.

Kurt walked over to a strange car and got in and drove off. Earlier in the month, Eric had purchased five used cars and had them stored in a local warehouse to be used for stakeouts. Kurt changed cars every evening to help prevent Art from knowing he was under constant surveillance. Carl would run a new car over to him whenever he called. Several times, he came out of a building and saw a different car parked where his old one had been. He knew Carl had traded cars for him while he was inside. The transfers seemed to be working. Art never knew he was being tailed or he never would have gone after Eric.

Chapter Thirty-five

Kurt was in the hall outside the operating room, standing next to Ann, when he saw Bertha rush in. She had tears in her eyes and he quickly assured her Eric was going to be all right. "What happened? No one will tell me anything. Did he have a heart attack?" she pleaded. She had prayed all the way, that it was not his heart. She could not take another loved one falling from a heart attack.

"No Bertha, Art shot him in the back," Kurt told her and caught her as she slumped to the ground. A nurse ran over and put her in a wheel chair. Ann stayed next to her until she regained consciousness. Kurt continued. "He is going to be all right. I promise you," and Ann murmured the same feelings. "I got a hold of Art before he could take aim again. The first shot went through him but didn't hit any bone as far as they know. He is in surgery right now and should be in recovery in the next hour."

The doctor picked a good time to come out of the operating room and over to Bertha. Ann had her arm around her. "Hi Bert, Ann!" he smiled at   the   two   women.   "I   understand   Mr.

Hoffermeister is a friend of yours. He came through better than expected. The bullet didn't hit any vital organs and went clean through. He takes good care of himself physically, and has that going for him. He is in recovery and should be in his room within the hour."

"See, I told you he would be all right," Kurt and Ann both said at the same time; more to hear themselves say it than to tell Bertha. Kurt had not been this scared since his lovely wife died.

"He will need to be careful for about a week, but I see no reason he should not be able to go home tomorrow. I'd like to keep him for a couple days but he is already telling me he wants to go home. He said he has a beautiful nurse there that will take good care of him," the doctor said smiling at Bertha.

"That he does," Kurt broke in. "When can we see him?"

"Give us a half hour and he will be in his room," the doctor told him and walked over to give orders to the nurse. He turned and said to Kurt, "I understand he has you to thank that he is alive," He said to Kurt.

"I was just there. It is too bad I wasn't five seconds earlier. If I had he wouldn't be in a recovery room," Kurt belittled himself.

"That I don't know, but they said you put pressure on the wound until the paramedics arrived and that definitely helped save his life," the doctor said as he walked away.

Bertha went over and hugged Kurt. "Thank you, thank you," she said. It seemed like an eternity to Bertha before they called them and allowed Eric visitors. Ann left and was headed for her husband's office to tell him the good news.

Bertha walked into Eric's room, saw that smile, and knew he was going to be all right. She did not care if the nurse or Kurt was standing there; she walked over and kissed Eric on the mouth long and passionately. He smiled up at her, "that was all most worth getting shot," he smiled again. "Did we get him?" he looked past her and asked Kurt.

"Yeah pal! He is behind bars and is not about to get out. The Chief will be there at the arraignment and is going to demand no bail. He is not about to let him slip through the cracks," Kurt told him, and went on to explain how the shooting went down. "He did what we expected but neither one of us thought he would go this far. I was only ten feet from him when he fired off the first bullet."

"He got off more than one shot; you must be getting slow," Eric smiled up at his friend.

"How can you two joke about such a thing? Do you realize how close I came to losing you? It sounds like you put yourself up as a decoy," Bert said, the tears starting to flow.

"Honey!" Eric said, reaching for her hand. "We knew I was the only one without a Cease and Desist order out on Art. We figured he would come after me, but we didn't think he would come after me and shoot me in the back. I don't like getting shot," he gave her that smile again.

"There was no way we would have put Eric in jeopardy if we had known Art was walking around armed, but at least he will be locked up for a good many years. It was obvious it was pre-meditated," Kurt said.

"Let's not talk about it anymore," Eric said to Kurt. "I'm fine and I'll be home for Christmas. We can have a peaceful Holiday and not worry about what Art is up too."

Hazel and Carl came rushing into his room. "We got here as soon as we heard. No one told us. We heard it on the news," Hazel told them.

"I'm sorry," Kurt said. "I should have called you but things have been happening so fast. I called earlier but you were not home. I didn't want to leave a message; your boss has been shot. We didn't know how serious his wound was and I wanted to wait until I knew before calling anyone."

"Thanks, I guess you did what you should have done. She has been a basket case getting here tonight. I can imagine how she would have been if you'd left that message," Carl smiled at Kurt.

"I'm glad you're here," Eric told them. "I'd like you to go to the office and turn the phones over to my cell phone. Then close the office and put a sign on the door that we will be closed until January fifteenth. We will have our Grand Opening then. I think we all need a rest and now we can do it safely."

"That sounds like a splendid idea, boss," Hazel told him. "I think Carl and I will go back to California for Christmas, and return with the remainder of our stuff. I know my folks will be glad to get rid of our junk they have been storing it for us. They might even want to come back with us for the Grand Opening. We better leave now and let you get some rest."

"Schlick, please call sis and let her know I am okay. They should be getting home from their trip down state. I don't want her finding out through the morning news," He smiled.

"I'll call right away. You get some rest and I'll be right back as soon as I reach her," Bertha told him, kissing him on the lips again before leaving the room. She hated to leave him for even a second.

Chapter Thirty-six

Three days later, Carl and Hazel flew out to visit her parents for Christmas. Kurt had two friends visit him from Mexico that day. They planned to stay over the Holidays and Bertha brought Eric home from the hospital.

Bertha set him up in her bedroom where he would be close to the bathroom. She would stay in the guestroom until he was able to go down to the lower level. The doctor said he should be able to move into his own room by Christmas Day.

Christmas Eve, Eric felt good enough to be up most of the day and Bertha fixed his favorite meal of scallop potatoes and ham. She laughed when he told her it was his favorite meal. "You can't get it at a restaurant," he complained. "They can fix fish, chicken or ham but for some reason they can't fix good scallop potatoes and ham."

That evening they had a Caesar salad with his favorite meal. After dinner, they sat before the fire on a large blanket and enjoyed a glass of wine.

Eric moved closer to Bertha and said, "I have something to tell you and I want you to take your time, answering me. I realize we have known each other less than a year but after this last scare, I want things set straight between us."

"Yes, what is it?" Bert said. "You're all right aren't you? You're not hiding something from me. Are you sure you're comfortable."

"Please! I'm not made of glass. I am not going to leave you any time soon. Hush, I just want you to know how much I love you. I guess I'm not doing too good a job at it. Maybe this will explain," he said reaching in his pocket and pulling out a ring box.

"Eric, I can't accept this," She said.

"Just wear it on your right hand until you decide you love me as much as I love you," he pleaded, pulling out a beautiful two-carat solitaire. "We will take it slow and easy. Just think about it," he added.

"Eric I am sure I feel very strongly about you, but I don't think I am ready to make this big a commitment yet," Bertha said. "I also don't know if I could take another evening like the evening last weekend."

"You could if we worked side by side. I can train you as my helper and we can work together. That way you can be sure I don't get into any more trouble. Bert, in all the years I've been doing this work; this is the first time I have ever been close to being shot," he tried to assure her.

"And you probably wouldn't have been shot this time if you had not been trying to protect me. I wanted Art found guilty of murder but not yours," Bert said and the tears began to show again in her eyes.

"Honey! I'm fine. He is just another sick-o. He actually convinced himself that if I was out of the way, he could get you for himself. We won't be running across many Art's. I can guarantee you that. Now please wear this and think about what I said. If you don't want me in six months, you can make a nice dinner ring out of it. Heck, I'll even have it made for you," he smiled.

"Eric, you're terrible. You know I can't resist you when you smile at me like that," she said and watched him put the ring on her right ring finger. She leaned over and accepted a long kiss from him.

They were in each other's arms when the doorbell rang. Bertha got up and looked out the window next to the door. "Honey, come here. We have carolers," she told him. She went back and helped him reluctantly get up, quickly folding up the fireplace blanket and tossing it over his back to keep him warm. She went to the door and opened it. Eric saw his parents standing on the porch. The small group began singing the minute Eric appeared in the doorway and his father's rich bass voice boomed out "Oh come all ye faithful."

"Mom, Dad, this is wonderful," he said and almost fell into his father's arms. He pulled them in out of the cold, with his good arm and kissed his mother as soon as she got to where he could reach her. His sister and brother-in-law were standing at the back of the porch and followed them into the house. "This is really great," Eric said for the forth time. "Mom! How did dad get you to come here in the winter?" He asked. Then turning he quickly said, "Oh, I'm sorry; Mom, dad, this is Schlick. She is my nurse and best friend." He placed his arm around Bert and led her over to his Mom and dad. "Bertha, this is Hattie and Bud, my Mom and Dad.

"It is so nice to finally meet you. Mary and Steve have talked about nothing else since we left the airport to come here. I can see why my son is so enamored with you," Eric's father said. He noticed his wife was giving Bert the once-over, from head to foot.

Hattie extended her hand to Bert and said, "Please call me Hattie," she told her.

Bert smiled at both of them as she accepted Hattie's outstretched hand. "Thank you and please call me Bert or Bertha; I answer to either. I've heard some wonderful things about you from your son. Please make yourself comfortable. I'll put a pot of tea on. Eric said that was your choice of beverage." She took the blanket from Eric and placed it on the back of the sofa.

"That would be very nice but allow me to help you," Hattie said.

Mary smiled to herself; she knew poor Bert was in for the third degree. "Mother, let me help her. You put your feet up and relax." She said this as she smiled at her Mom.

"Thank you dear, but I need to walk around for a little while. That plane trip was a real drag on these old joints," Hattie told her daughter and followed Bert to the kitchen. "What can I do to help?" she asked Bert.

"Make sure I fix your tea the way you like it. I am not very good at it," Bert told her.

"I'm sure it will be fine. I understand there is not very much you're not good at, including making my son fall head over heels in love with you," Hattie said. She continued, "I understand you don't feel the same about him." She paused, waiting for Bert to answer.

"That's not true. I'm pretty crazy about him too. You have a wonderful son."

One to speak what was on her mind, Hattie said, "then why won't you marry him?"

"I have only been a widow for a very short time and there are other reasons," Bert told her.

"Your age difference; don't look so shocked. You might know he told us everything. You don't look older than my son. Did you know I was also a widow when I married Eric's father and I'm older than Eric's father by Ten years?" Hattie emphasized the statement. "These Hoffermeister men like their women a little older."

"Eric never told me," Bert said.

"That is because Eric doesn't pay any attention to the ages of people. He has had younger bimbo's and that is just what they were. He soon tired of them and has been a very lonely man for many years," Hattie told her. "I don't think there is anything that bothers a mother more than seeing her son lonely unless it is seeing him shot."

Bert felt a twang going through her heart. That woman really knew how to reach a person. She is as bad as her son is, Bert thought. She is reading me like a book.

Just then Mary; not wanting to wait any longer, walked into the kitchen. "Have you finished giving Bert the third degree?" She smiled at her mother.

"Yes, you timed it beautifully dear," Hattie returned her smile, "and I hope I've straightened her out on a few things she was not aware of," Hattie smiled at Bert and walked back into the living room. She smiled at her son and gave him a wink of her eye. He knew she had told Bert about herself and his father. He hoped it might make a difference.

"Dad and I would like to stay here a few days, if that is all right. Just until you get some of your strength back. I could spank your sister for not telling us you had been shot; and in the back yet," Hattie said.

"You're more than welcome I'm sure," he told his mother. "Bert has another room right next to mine in the lower level and the way dad has trouble sleeping; there is a living area with a fine big television. You'll like my apartment. It is almost as big as my house was in California. Come on down and I'll show you around," He said. The three of them went down to the lower level.

Bertha saw them leave and frowned. She did not like the way Eric looked. She was afraid he had over done it today.

"Did she push too much, Bert?" Mary asked. "Mom has a habit of speaking her mind."

"No, she was very gracious but I don't like the look of Eric. He looks terribly tired," Bert told her. "Your mother was very kind. She as much as told me; I have her approval. I wonder how she will feel when she finds out Eric took a bullet from someone that was really after me," Bert continued.

"She already knows. We told her on the way here from the airport," Mary answered.

.   "She still came," Bert said surprised.

"Yes, all she said was; that poor woman. She must have been scared to death. It's a good thing Eric was there to protect her," Mary told Bert.

"She is one different lady. I'm afraid if I had a son, I would not be as generous toward someone that almost got him killed," Bertha said.

"That's just Mom. She is one of a kind," Mary said. "Come on; let's go see what they are up to. Steve is taking their suitcases down. They must have approved of their living arrangements," Mary laughed.

They were more than pleased. Eric was lying on the sofa, after his father insisted he help him down the stairs to the lower level. Eric was watching Steve kill Budd in a game of pool and Hattie was encouraging Budd not to give up. They laughed and enjoyed several games; changing partners every time they finished a game. When it was Bert and Hattie's turn to face off with Budd and Steve, they cleared the table and smiled demurely at the men and Hattie asked, "Would you gentlemen like a few lessons?" They all laughed.

Chapter Thirty-seven

Hattie and Bertha baked and cooked Christmas morning, taking their goodies over to Mary and Steve's for what was to become an annual Christmas dinner. Mary really out did herself. She had turkey, ham, salmon, mashed potatoes, gravy, sweet potatoes, lima beans, and several other side dishes. Bert brought the Waldorf salad, four pies, two pumpkins and two apples. Bert also brought cranberries; fresh baked rolls and lots of whipped cream. They all ate too much and decided to have dessert later that evening at Bertha's. Bertha smiled knowing she would have to take all the deserts back home.

Bertha received a call from Max before they left for Mary and Steve's, telling her that Elizabeth had eaten something that did not agree with her, so they would not be up for a couple days. He wished her a Merry Christmas and told her not to worry. They would see them by the end of the week.

Presents were distributed one at a time. Each person had to un-wrap his or her gift before the next person could open theirs. Eric's parents were pleased with the small portable grill that closed up to a very small package so they could take it home with them. Bert had purchased it when Eric told her they needed one. He had not realized she had bought it and had it under Mary and Steve's tree, waiting for their arrival. Bert received a beautiful scarf, sock cap and gloves; Hattie had knitted for her. She had a matching set for each of her children and her son-in-law. "I think Mom is under the assumption we get a little cold up here," Mary laughed.

"I do," Bertha said thanking Hattie, "and I'll really put these to good use."

They left Mary and Steve's later that day to go to Bert's for a quick nap. Mary said she and Steve would do the same and meet them later. Eric needed the rest and the only way to get him to lie down was if they all did; so as soon as they entered the house they all went to their rooms. Eric was sleeping a half-hour later when the rest of the family met in the living room to talk.

Around seven o'clock he woke and Bert fixed coffee and tea and served the dessert. They sang Christmas Carol's and Bertha played her guitar. Steve brought his and between the two of them, the music rolled throughout the house. The high ceilings made their voices even sweeter and they could be heard outside when Eric and Budd slipped out on the front porch for some air and a few minutes of father, son talk.

When they returned Budd said, "This has been one of the nicest Christmas's I can remember. Thank you so much, Bertha. Steve doesn't play for us often, and having the two of you playing and singing together, has been a real treat. The guitar is one thing I have always wanted to learn to play but I don't have the patience. Steve tried to help me once but we both agreed I was a lost cause," he laughed.

Hattie hunched her shoulders and yawned, "Well! Since I have such a beautiful room to retire in, that is exactly what I am about to do. It has been a long day and I am terribly tired. I'll see you all in the morning," She kissed her husband goodnight and went over to Bert. "Thank you so much dear, you are a very gracious hostess. I feel very much at home here," She gave Bert a peck on the cheek and left for her room. Eric walked over and gave his mother a hug and kiss as she went down the stairs.

Everyone called it an early evening and Steve and Mary went home about an hour later. Budd went down to his room and said goodnight to Bertha and his son. Eric had insisted on staying behind. He said he wanted to help Bertha put the dishes in the dishwasher. She was leaning over the dishwasher taking the dishes he handed her when she said, "Your mother and father are wonderful. I can see how it would have been great to have them as parents." Straightening up she added, "It's no wonder you grew up to be the man you are, with their guidance. You must have been the joy of their lives."

"I was a brat," Eric confided in her. "I did all the things boys do, and then added a few of my own. There was more than a few times my dad had to have a father-son conference. I usually came away with a sore hind-end for a few hours," he laughed.

"Your dad spanked you?" Bert asked.

"Yes and more than once. Believe me, I had it coming," Eric told her.

"He doesn't look the type to raise a hand against a child," Bert was astonished.

"Hey! Dad didn't beat me. He just swatted me on the butt. It was better than when I grew older. He took the keys to the car away from me and put me on a curfew," Eric protested.

"You must have been a handful," Bert laughed.

"That's what I've been trying to tell you. Whatever they did, they did it right. I don't sass my folks anymore. I don't smoke and I don't drink to excess, I believe in God and I have always tried, in later years, to make them proud of me," Eric told her.

"I'm sure you have, dear. You mother beams when she talks about you and your dad can't say enough about your accomplishments," Bert assured him.

"You three must have talked all afternoon, while I slept. It's a wonder my ears didn't burn off," Eric teased.

"We did enough that if you still want me to marry you; I'm more than willing," Bert said and took off her ring and handed to him to place on her left ring finger.

Eric looked down at her and said, "Before you get Elizabeth's permission?"

"I don't need my daughter's permission. I am going to do what my heart tells me. I would like it to be a long engagement though," Bert told him.

"How ever long you want it," he said and put the ring on its proper finger. "Right now you can have as long an engagement as you think necessary." When they finished kissing, he asked, "How long?

"Is six months to a year, too long?" she asked hoping he would agree.

"Yes! I'll take what I can get and hope it is six months," he smiled at her. "Now, my little prize, I am going to bed while I am still the gentleman you think I am," he smiled that smile.

She kissed him and he left for the lower level. She went to her room and before she fell asleep, she had already decided a year was too long.

Chapter Thirty-eight

Elizabeth and Max arrived the next day. She was apologetic about getting sick and missing Christmas.

"That's okay dear. Eric's parents are here and I put you and Max in the spare room up here with me," Bertha told her.

"Is he still here, and now he's moved his folks in?" Elizabeth questioned.

"Yes, for a little while. He will be moving into his place as soon as his wound is healed sufficiently," She told her daughter.

"Wound, WHAT wound?" Elizabeth cried.

Bertha explained the last week and a half to Elizabeth and watched her daughter's face turn a chalky white.

"Mother Schlinkenmayer, why didn't you let us know?" Max asked; putting one arm around his shocked wife and his other arm around Bertha.

"I was in good hands, as you can see and I didn't want to worry you unnecessarily. I am just sorry Eric got shot trying to solve Nancy's murder. Now let's change the subject and get you two settled. Eric and his parents should be back within the hour and we will all go to the club. I for one am getting tired of turkey," Bertha laughed.

Eric came back without his parents. "The folks are going to meet us at the club for dinner. Mom didn't think she had been spending enough time with Mary so they dropped me off and went over to Mary and Steve's," he told Bertha.

Max and Elizabeth came into the kitchen when they heard Eric's voice. "Hey, old man! I understand we owe you a debt of gratitude. Mother said you saved her life," Max said, giving his friend a hug.

"Not really, I was the one he was really after. He wanted your mother to himself for some serious love making," Eric smiled at Bert.

"Ugh! Don't even kid about that. He turns my stomach and I would like to have a nice meal tonight. What time are we to meet the rest of the group?" Bert asked changing the subject.

"I thought I'd take a nap and we would go over about six. If that's okay with the rest of you," Eric said.

"Good idea," Max said and watched Eric slowly walk down the stairs. When Eric was all the way into the lower level, Max said, "He doesn't look like the old Eric. What do the doctors say about his recovery?" he asked Bert. Max really liked Eric and hated to see him looking and moving like an old man.

"They told him to take it easy for the next month or so but you know him. His folks came and we all celebrated Christmas and then of course he had to show them the office and his new house. What he needs now is rest. He's supposed to sleep at least an hour every afternoon. I am happy to see he is at least following those orders," Bert told them.

"Then we will make sure he does," Elizabeth said. She could not believe the difference in Eric's appearance. He looked older than her mother did.

Eric appeared in the living room doorway at five thirty. He looked a hundred percent better then he had when he went downstairs. He had taken a long nap, showered and put on the sweater and slack outfit Bertha had bought him for Christmas. He looked even better in it than she envisioned he would. They both fit him perfectly. The light yellow turtleneck sweater was definitely his color and set his sparkling brown eyes off. The tan Cords were a nice match with his brown dress boots.

"You sure look better friend," Max told him. "I was a little worried you might be over doing it."

"No chance for that. Schlick keeps close tabs on me," He smiled. "Shall we leave for dinner," he suggested.

They all went in Max's car and arrived as Eric's family was being seated at a long table in the restaurant area. Eric quickly introduced his parents to Elizabeth. They recognized Max, and immediately started talking about old times. Some of the things those men did together when they were younger, made everyone laugh outrageously.

"It wasn't nearly as funny then as it is now," Hattie said. "It seemed like what one didn't think of to get them into trouble, the other one did. You'll have your hands full," She said to Bert and

Hattie took her left hand, giving it a gentle squeeze. Just long enough to let Bertha know she noticed her son's ring was now on the proper finger.

Not missing anything, Elizabeth gave her mother a questioning look. She had noticed the ring earlier, but had not paid much attention to it. She thought it might be one of those fake diamonds Mom was always buying and using as her latest dinner ring, but now taking a closer look she noted it was real and it was an engagement ring; a pretty impressive one too. Bertha looked at her daughter and smiled, whispering she would talk to her later.

"You certainly will," her daughter smiled sweetly at her mother.

Chapter Thirty-nine

Bertha was not happy to have the evening end; she knew her daughter was going to be upset, but to her surprise; Elizabeth merely said, "Mother, I am so happy for you, but how will Eric feel being married to a grandmother."

"What! Oh my, you're pregnant?" Bert asked excitedly.

"So they tell me. How would you like to be a grandma of twins?" Elizabeth smiled at her mother.

"I couldn't be happier and I know Eric will be as pleased as I. We are probably too old to have children and this way we can have the best of both worlds. We can have babies to spoil and then send them home to their parents," Bertha was smiling at her daughter as she gave her a big hug and kiss. "Where is that man of yours? I have to congratulate him?" She added.

"He'll be in as soon as he gets rid of some of the snow in the drive. He wanted to do some snow blowing before he drove all over the drive again. He said if he didn't do it, Eric would try, and he had no business in his condition, to even start the snow-blower," Elizabeth told her. "And don't count yourself out. Eric may have other ideas about children."

Bertha smiled and thought, from your mouth to God's ears. She would love to give Eric a child, but merely answered her daughter, "Of course, Max is right. Budd offered to do it tomorrow morning but I told him I had a man that would come over to clear the drive," Bertha told her.

"Let Max clear the snow. He wanted some exercise and Budd and Eric said they would keep him company. From what Max told me about Eric's father, he will want to take a turn at the snow-blower," Elizabeth told her mother.

"You're so right," Hattie said as she walked up from downstairs.

"Let's at least make some hot cocoa for them. They will want something hot to drink when they come in," Bertha said. She stopped talking and turned pale. She was listening to the news. Arthur Plant had escaped from the hospital after being sent there with what the prison doctor diagnosed as a possible appendicitis attack the newscaster said. Bertha went to the door and called the men inside. They wanted to finish but she insisted. They knew she must have an important reason for calling them in. When they took off their boots and gloves and walked into the back hall, Bertha was there with tears in her eyes. She stood in the doorway without a coat or hat and looked chilled to the bone. She was not going to let them out of her sight until she saw all the men safely inside the house. By the time they turned off the snow blower and walked in, she was in tears.

"What is it darling? What is wrong?" Eric asked. Bertha told him and they all went into the living room; the men were still wearing their snow gear.

"It can't be that bad. How long before they found him missing?" Eric kept questioning the television as if it was going to answer him. Hearing they had no idea where Art disappeared to, Eric went over to the phone and called the police department.

They talked for several minutes and when he hung up the phone, he went out to the security system and engaged it.

Entering the living room he said, "Come out to the laundry room Dad and Mom, I want to show you how to use the security system." They followed him in and he said, "We will leave the system on (stay) and not turn it off for any reason unless we leave the house. Then we will put it on (away)," he told them. "I've bi-passed the lower level motion detector so we can walk around freely, but all the doors are wired.

He had them both set and reset the system so they would be familiar with it. After he was satisfied, he put the system back on (stay) and led them back to the living room. Elizabeth and her husband already knew how to turn it off and on.

"I don't think we have too much to worry about. Art is probably into Canada by now but if he isn't, they will find him. We can still enjoy the remainder of our Holiday. We won't let him ruin the few days we have left," He told his Mom and

Dad. "Come on, I can smell the cocoa. Let's all have some." He sounded much more confident than he really felt. How anyone could let a murderer walk out of a hospital was beyond his reasoning. He knew there was more to it than he heard over the news or by the police officer that answered the phone when he called headquarters. He put in a call to the Chief of Police's cell phone and left a message. He would wait until he heard from him before doing anything.

Bertha poured hot chocolate for everyone and put a new batch on the stove to heat. She wanted to stay busy. She did not want to think about Arthur Plant; much less, what he might do.

Gary and Kurt arrived in the drive at the same time and walked up to the front door together. The Chief was so apologetic you would have thought it was his fault Art had escaped. "I had two men on him but when he went into the operating room, they were not allowed past the door. Art struck the doctor before they could put him to sleep and held a knife to the surgical nurse, using her as a shield. They said all the signs show he won't get far. With appendicitis, he will be very ill within a couple days so he will need medical help," Gary told the group.

"I wouldn't put anything past him," Kurt said. "He has slipped between the fingers of more than one police department. "He may not even have appendicitis."

"He had all the signs of a ruptured appendix," Gary argued.

"Yeah! One time he was such a good actor the doctors said he had suffered a stroke. I'm telling you that guy is no sicker than I am. You better keep a guard on this house, the office and the border crossings. He might slip across until he figures the heat is off him," Kurt warned.

"I haven't told you all of it," Gary said.

"Let's have it. I hope it is not bad news," Kurt said.

"No! I heard from the California coroner. His first wife was murdered with a very rare poison. She was unconscious when she drowned. The coroner tried to get the chief to let him work on the case but he was told he had more pressing cases to handle so he closed the file on her and released the body to Art. He wanted her cremated but her relatives stepped in and demanded she be buried in the family plot. Art didn't like it but he didn't want to make too many waves."

"He probably was worried if he did, they might get suspicious," Kurt said.

"Yeah! They would have if it were not for the fact Art was so upset by her death; he gave her a huge funeral. Complete with music and hundreds of flowers. That's about all I know for the moment. "I'll let you people enjoy what's left of your evening. I want to get back to headquarters and find out if they have heard anything," Gary said

. Eric knew Gary could have called and found out if there were any late developments but he thanked the chief for stopping in and walked him to the door.

A strange car was parked across the street in the driveway at the doctor's house. Eric knew the doctor was not in residence. He noticed Gary walk over and talk to the men in the front seat. Erik took two thermoses of cocoa out to the men and handed them a large bag of Bert's cookies. The two men smiled and thanked him. Eric walked back to the house and set the system again.

The surveillance went on for two weeks and then Eric called it off. If Art had not been heard from for two weeks or even spotted, it was a sure bet he was long gone.

Everything seemed to quiet down, and they all enjoyed a peaceful week before Eric's parents returned home, but not before they made plans to spend part of the summer with Eric. Working together before their departure, they helped Eric move most of his things to his new home. He had sold all his furnishings with his California house so he and Bert would have to do a lot of shopping before he would be able to get settled in permanently.

Chapter Forty

It had been four months since anyone had heard anything from Art. The police had run out of ideas and leads. Life was getting back to normal.

Bert had a ball furnishing Eric's new home. He would not purchase as much as a washcloth without her approval. They found him a beautiful oak, sleigh bed, large triple dresser with matching nightstands and an armoire'. His living room had the two, burgundy leather recliners Bert had shipped up with Kurt's, and had been stored in her old exercise room in the lower level all this time. The carpets throughout were in mauve. The remainder of his main room was gray and mauve with green accents. She called his kitchen every woman's dream. He had purchased every appliance possible and beautiful china, pots, pans, and linens. The flatware took him a little longer. He had too many choices to choose from. Bert told him either that or he didn't want to finish and move out of her home, but two months after Christmas he was settled in his new digs.

They still saw each other constantly. She was in training and he took her everywhere.

When they were not working together, they were either at his house or at Bert's.

Bertha began to worry. She could not put off marrying Eric much longer and she thought it might be a good time for her to go and see her daughter. She wanted to make sure everything was all right with her pregnancy and she was not working too hard. Eric did not like her going alone but she had deliberately chosen a time she knew he could not get away from his work.

She went down to Plymouth and directly to her daughter's bookstore. Elizabeth was not there. Her assistant told Bertha her boss had not expected her before dinner so she took the afternoon off to do some shopping. Bertha had a key to her daughter's home so she drove out to Colony Farms and let herself in.

To Bert's surprise, Elizabeth was there, taking a nap. She heard someone enter and called out, "Is that you, Max?"

"No dear, it's mother. May I come in?" she asked her while standing outside her bedroom door.

"Of course, mother. I was just about to get up. I thought I might lie down for a few minutes before going shopping and must have been more tired than I thought. Oh my," Elizabeth said. "I've been sleeping for two hours. It's time I got up. I'm glad you came early or I might have slept all afternoon."

"It is good for you to get plenty of rest. I see I need not have worried about you. You seem to be taking good care of yourself. How are the babies?" Bertha asked.

"The doctor said they couldn't be in a better position or healthier at this stage of my pregnancy. They both have strong heart beats," Elizabeth told her mother. "It looks like I am going to have an easy time of it; like my mother I hope," she concluded and rose to give her a kiss and hug.

Bertha did not know when she loved her daughter more than at this minute. She gave her a gentle hug and said, "I thought I would give Eric a week or so to change his mind. I hope you don't mind the company. We might shop for grandma gifts, if you feel up to it."

"I'd love to. I know you said you and Eric wanted to buy the baby's beds so I have been holding off shopping for any furniture. Can we go tomorrow or do you have other plans?" Elizabeth asked. She knew Bertha would have to see several of her friends while she was down state. She always had several luncheon engagements set up before she arrived.

"No, dear, my time is your time. I have no other plans other than you and the babies," Bert smiled.

Elizabeth took her mother to Max's office and he treated them all to dinner at Bert's favorite Italian restaurant on Plymouth Road. She had her usual Eggplant Lasagna and laughed when she could not finish it. "You never finish it Mom. We will take it home for your lunch tomorrow. I will make me a salad and after lunch we'll go shopping.

Chapter Forty-one

The two women went shopping the next day and Bertha bought several skeins of yarn. She did not like any of the little sweater outfits for her new grandchildren and decided to knit them herself. She also bought material to make her daughter some cute maternity smocks.

They were busy sewing when Max came home. "Mother, what are you up too?" He asked. "I've bought enough outfits for Elizabeth to last her through two pregnancies. She knows if there is anything she needs she only has to tell me."

"Honey! Mom is making me some things I couldn't find. She is a whiz at that machine you bought me. I've learned more about the mechanics of the thing than I could have learned in a month of lessons. Now I won't need lessons. We have had a great time. Look at the little bib overhauls Mom showed me how to make. They are just like the ones she made for me when I first started walking. I'll have them for the babies when they play outside next summer," Elizabeth said excitedly.

Max smiled, "You're getting a little ahead of yourself, aren't you dear. We don't know if they are boys or girls yet and it looks like they better be boys," He said admiring the little trousers. "Honey, I haven't seen you this interested in anything since we furnished this house."

Elizabeth went over to her husband and gave him a big hug. "If you're good, I might make you a matching pair of overhauls," she teased. "Come on, let's get some dinner started," she said, taking his arm and moving out of the workroom.

"Why don't I take my lovely ladies to the restaurant downtown that has the great fish? You haven't had your fish this week," Max told her as they walked down the stairs."

"Your getting to be a real health food nut; do you know that?" she laughed. "But we will take you up on dinner out," she told him and turned to tell her mother to close up the sewing machine for tonight. "Max is going to take us to dinner again."

"You don't need to call me twice. My neck is telling me I haven't worked this hard at a sewing machine in a long time. Let me go in and freshen up a little. I'll be down shortly," Bertha said.

They had dinner and by the time they got home everyone was tired, so after an hour of television they retired for the evening.

Bert went up to her room. She had refused the master bedroom and was very comfortable in the large guestroom. She turned and tossed all evening. She had not called Eric and knew she should have at least tried and left a message she would be gone all day. That was not all that bothered her. She was always looking behind her expecting to see Art in the shadows. How in the world will she ever get him to crawl out of the woodwork? She had an idea but she could not tell anyone but Eric. Elizabeth and Max did not need to know anything about what she planned. They had enough on their minds right now and why spoil their excitement over the babies expected arrivals.

The next morning she awoke and found Elizabeth standing over her with a cup of coffee. "You shouldn't be serving me coffee in bed, silly. You should be the one being served," Bert told her.

"You were sleeping so soundly, I was worried about you. Do you feel okay?" Elizabeth asked.

"Yes, of course. I didn't get to sleep till well past midnight. My mind would not shut down," Bert said.

"Did you make up your mind about anything? I know you have been trying to decide when you will marry Eric," her daughter asked.

"I think we will make it sometime in August. The twins should be able to travel by then. You traveled when you were only five and a half weeks old. In truth, you were the only one that had a good time. Your father and I almost melted in the heat," Bertha laughed.

"The doctor said they should arrive somewhere around June 4th. July or August would be fine with us. When are Eric's parents expected back?" she asked.

"Probably sometime in May. They plan to stay the summer. They have rented a place in Michaywe'. They know about the twins and Hattie is almost as excited as I am. She is a remarkable woman. You can expect a lot of homemade items from her. I know she is knitting furiously," Bertha smiled. "Well dear, if you think August is not too soon after the baby's birth that is when we will plan it. I'll talk to Eric. I know he will be excited to finally have a definite date," Bert laughed.

Chapter Forty-two

Bertha was back on the road a week later, heading for home. She drove up to the office and Eric heard her voice as she entered and was greeting the receptionist. He almost fell getting down the stairs.

"You didn't tell me you were coming home today," He said.

"I can leave again if it is not convenient," she teased.

"Come here Schlick," he said, reaching for her. She went willingly into his arms and he kissed her right there in the reception area. Luckily, no one was there but Kathy. He took her hand and smiled that smile. "Come on," he said. "I'll take you to lunch."

"I haven't had a better offer in days," Bertha smiled back at him and he took her hand and led her out of the building.

After they were seated at the restaurant, he inquired. "So what do I owe this pleasant surprise; maybe you missed me as much as I missed you."

"That's about it, and the fact I have been worrying about Art again," Bertha told him.

"Well! Stop worrying about that guy. He is long gone," He tried to assure her.

"I think you're wrong. I know he will be back and I am tired of waiting for him to pop up one day. I think we ought to find a way to bring him out in the open," Bertha told Eric.

"I've been thinking along the same lines. See how good we are for one another. We even think alike. My only trouble is; I can't decide how to do it," Eric told her.

"I think I have a good idea. Now, please wait and hear me out," Bertha said. Eric frowned at her but waited patiently for her to finish. "I think, once we announce our engagement and the date of the wedding; he will show up."

"I'm not sure I like that idea. Don't get me wrong. I've been kicking around a similar idea for weeks and I'll take any date you'll give me, but it sounds like we might be setting you up as a decoy," Eric told her.

"No, I think you will be the decoy. He will either try to kidnap me or go after you again. I don't like that part even a little bit, but I see no other way. We can't live our life worrying about when he will try to get at one of us. We wanted to set a date for the wedding and if he doesn't show so much the better. At least we will know we are rid of him and we can stop looking behind us constantly," Bertha told him.

"You're right. We will know one way or the other. What date do you have in mind? Is tomorrow too soon," He teased.

"Behave yourself and let's decide on sometime in August." She explained Elizabeth and Max would be able to be here with the babies by then.

"Too bad they won't be old enough to take grandma and grandpa down the aisle," He smiled and squeezed her hand.

"You two look very pleased with yourselves," Kim, the waitress said as she delivered their meals.

"We are; Bert finally decided we would be married in August," He told Kim.

"It's about time. If she didn't hurry up, I and half the girls here were going to thrash her," she smiled. "Enjoy," she said and left their table. As usual, they didn't see her again until she brought them the check. She was always so busy she seldom had time to chat. "Who are you going to have catering your reception?" Kim took time to ask.

"Probably the clubhouse but we would like you and your Mom to cater the engagement party at my home, if that is convenient," Bertha told her.

"You get me a date and we will be there. Right now, August looks pretty clear, but the sooner I know the better," She smiled and said, "Lunch is on me. We will call it the announcement luncheon."

"She must be pleased for us," Bertha said as Kim went to another table. "This is the first time I've ever heard of her giving away a meal," Bertha smiled. "Well sir, we better get you back to work. You have been slacking off long enough and I am sure Hazel will want to leave for lunch."

"She already has. Carl picked her up just before you arrived. They had some shopping to do and I told her to take the afternoon off. I think they went to Traverse City," he told her.

They went back to the office and Bertha suggested Kathy go get herself some lunch, she would take over the phones while she was gone. Kathy thanked her and left immediately.

"I'll sit down here and keep you company," Eric leered at Bertha.

"No you won't. I know you are swamped with the Ellery case and I don't want to distract you," Bert told him. "Why don't you come for dinner tonight and we can talk some more. Now scoot, the phone is ringing and I'll bet it is for you."

He waited while she answered and heard her say, "Yes, Kurt I'm back. I'm just filling in for Kathy while she goes to lunch. Yes! He is right here. Give him a minute and I'll transfer your call to his office." She nodded at Eric and he climbed the stairs to his private office and closed the door. She transferred the phone call and answered several others before Kathy returned. "Do these phones ever stop ringing," she smiled at Kathy as she entered the building.

"Sometimes I sit here for a couple hours and then everyone wants to call at once," she smiled back. "I'll take over now. You've had a long day, why don't you go home and relax," Kathy suggested.

Bertha smiled back at her, went up to Eric's office and peered into the room. "I'll see you about six thirty," She said. He nodded and went back to what he was doing. She closed his door, walked back downstairs and went out to her car.

She did as Kathy suggested and went directly home. Bertha pulled some things from the freezer, went to her room and promptly fell asleep on top of the quilt on her bed. If she had not gotten chilly about an hour and a half later, she probably would have slept through the dinner hour.

Chapter Forty-three

Eric arrived at precisely six thirty bearing a large bouquet of roses. He handed her the flowers and gave her a peck on the cheek. "I thought these might brighten up the place. I don't know how I lived alone so long. I've really missed living here. I came in to water your flowers and as lovely as your home is; it was too quiet and cold. Your being in it is what gives it life," Eric told her.

"Thank you kind sir; that is possibly the nicest things anyone has said to me in a long time,"she smiled and walked over to where he was sitting and gave his head a hug, leaning down, she buzzed his cheek. "I'll have dinner ready soon. Would you like a glass of wine before we eat?"

"No thanks, I just want to sit and watch you, if you don't mind. That kitchen was made for you. You move around like you really are enjoying it," He said.

"I am, my Uncle Jerry designed it and he knew what he was doing. I told you he used to sell kitchen cabinets and this was one of the last kitchens he did before retiring. I don't know what I'll do if I ever need another one," She said. "I am amazed how beautiful your kitchen turned out. It was also designed to be convenient for the cook."

"I have a secret. I called your uncle and sent him my plans. He was the one that designed it. I hoped some day you would be cooking there and it should be to your liking. Jerry said that would be our wedding gift," Eric smiled that smile.

Bertha could not help herself. She went back over to him and this time she planted a big kiss on his mouth. "You do some of the nicest thing. That is just one of them," she said. He pulled her down on his lap and she sat there comfortable until she heard the timer call her. She reluctantly got up and went back to the kitchen.

They ate their dinner in relatively silence. Eric said it was the best meal he had since she left.

After the dishes were cleared, placed in the dishwasher; they went into the living room for coffee. She never had cooking utensils to do after a meal as she always washed them up as she went. She disliked having to clean pots and pans after she had just enjoyed a nice meal.

They talked for several minutes and Bertha asked, "What did Kurt have to say?"

"He's finished up his case load and wanted to know what our plans were. He would like to go down to Mexico for a week or so, and do some fishing along the way. I told him he had until July but in July, August and September, I want him to stay close and handle the office," Eric said.

"Why July, August, and September? I can see part of August, but three months?" She questioned.

"You don't think you are going to have all the fun planning our wedding, do you, so that takes care of July. August is set aside for our wedding and September is for our honeymoon. I have somewhere special I want to take you," Eric told her.

"Are you going to let me in on it," Bert asked.

"No! If I did, it wouldn't be a surprise," He smiled. "Now, shall we announce August fourth?" Eric asked. "That is pretty close to my birthday."

"That is so I won't have too many dates to remember," she teased.

"You'd never forget my birthday. It is too close to yours," he teased back.

"Seriously dear, that was my dad's birthday and I'm sure he would look down on us and be pleased we picked that day."

"Then the fourth of August it is. You really believe he is looking down on you, don't you?" he said.

"Yes! He and Mom have been my guardian angles since they died. How else could I have survived some of the things I've been through," She said. She did not mention what things, but Eric knew she was thinking of her parents' untimely death, her grandparents leaving this earth the following year, and Jeff's sudden heart attack; not to mention old Art.

"Let's work on the announcement. We won't put it in the paper until Kurt gets back. We want him around to guard our backs, just in case," Eric told her.

They worked on the announcement and when she had typed the final draft into her computer, Eric excused himself and went to his home.

They both slept better than either one had in over a week.

Chapter Forty-four

Kurt arrived the following week and was thrilled they had finally agreed on a date for their wedding. "I don't know how pleased I am about you two making yourselves decoys for old Art, but I will make sure he doesn't get too close to you this time."

"We know friend," Eric told him. "How about dinner tonight at the clubhouse, my treat."

"How can I refuse," Kurt laughed.

They closed up the office at six and the three of them headed for the clubhouse. When they walked in, there was Eric's favorite hostess. He smiled and she showed them to a table immediately. "See it pays to be nice to the help," he smiled at Bert.

"Just so you know who you really belong to," Bert scolded.

"You two sound like an old married couple already. When is the announcement appearing in the paper?" Kurt asked.

"This next week. The announcement and our picture will appear in the Detroit News and Free Press on the weekend and all the local papers throughout the state. If he is anywhere around, he is bound to see the nuptial announcement. Then all we do is wait. If he doesn't show up by August fourth, so much the better," Eric commented.

"You better hope he does, or you'll be taking me on your honeymoon," Kurt laughed.

"Forget it pal. I haven't even told Schlick where we are going," Kurt laughed.

"You should let someone know, just in case," Kurt suggested.

"I plan on letting you run things while we are away. I'll call you when we get where we are going and leave a number for you to contact us, but only if it is an emergency," Eric smiled at Bertha.

The announcement was in the papers that week and when next they visited the club the manager walked over with a bottle of champagne.

Congratulations, you finally got Bertha to say yes," he smiled at them. "Complements of the house," he said opening the bottle and pouring them each a glass.

"Please join us," Eric smiled, sliding out a chair.

"Thank you," Jeff replied and went over and got another Champaign glass. Eric poured Jeff a glass and the three talked about the coming nuptials. Another Jeff in Bertha's life, Eric thought to himself.

"We want the reception held here. Would you please have your girl call me so we can plan the menu," Bert told him.

"I'll be happy to and in the mean time; I'll reserve the big hall for you. With all the people you know, I just hope it will be large enough." Jeff laughed.

"We are asking not to have gifts sent. If they want to do something in our name to their favorite charity; we will appreciate it more," Eric said.

Just as they were finishing they heard a familiar voice. "What the heck," Eric said, leaping from the table. He dashed out to the reservation desk to find the head waitress very upset. "Was that who I think it was?" He questioned.

"Yes and I told him to get out," she said.

"Which way did he go?" Eric asked.

"He had a car waiting with the engine running. He wanted to know if you were here," she said.

"What did you tell him?" Eric asked.

"I told him I hadn't seen you. Which is the truth? I just came on my shift and didn't know who was here," she said.

"Please get on the phone and call the chief of police and tell him what just happened. I'll use my cell phone to call in some help," he told the woman. Eric called Kurt and told him what had just happened.

"I knew I shouldn't have left you go to dinner alone. Stay right there and I'll come and pick you up. I suggest we get some things from your place and the two of us stay at Bertha's tonight," Kurt said.

"You'll get no argument from me," Eric told him. He walked back to his table and found Jeff still seated with Bertha. "Thank you for waiting," he told Jeff. "If he comes in again, try to detain him and have someone call the police. He has warrants out for his arrest from California to Michigan. They believe he killed his wife in California a few years before he killed Nancy."

"He's been one busy devil, hasn't he? Why the one in California?" Jeff asked.

"Money! The same reason he killed Nancy. He got rich off the one out west and stashed the money somewhere while he went through most of Nancy's money. When he found out she was about to divorce him, he didn't want to part with the little she had left."

"Nancy was one of the finest women I've ever met. I hope they string him up," Jeff said as Kurt walked in.

"Get away from those windows," Kurt declared as he rushed into the restaurant. "Eric you know better. He could still be lurking around outside. Let's get the little lady home," he told him.

For the next couple of weeks Eric and Kurt never left Bertha out of their sight. It began to get on her nerves. When Eric hired two new agents, Sally and Don Benjamin, she begged him to let her and Hazel go with the new woman to lunch. He finally agreed and Hazel, Bertha and Sally left for a long, long, lunch.

They noticed Eric and Don sneak into the room later and take seats facing their booth. They all had the famous salad bar and Bertha ate better than she had in weeks. They talked, laughed and had a wonderful time. "As long as they are watching us, let's do some shopping," Bertha suggested.

"I better let my boss know," Sally said. "He pays my salary," she laughed and went over to their booth and told the men where their next stop would be. They did not look too excited but Eric knew there were some things Bertha wanted before the wedding and the time seemed to be slipping by. He and Don would tag along at a safe distance. When the women left they drove Don's car and followed along behind. The women did not say they were going to shop! Shop! Before too long, both Don and Eric's feet were telling them it was time to go back to the office.

Eric walked over to Bertha, put his arm around her and said, "Okay honey, we get the message. We can't keep up; let's go back to the office."

She smiled and told him to give them ten more minutes and they would be ready too. "I need to go to Traverse City for the other things I need," she told him. "I just don't want you to go with us."

Eric tried to look hurt but smiled and said, "If you don't want my company at least take Don and Kurt with you. I'll set something up for tomorrow."

She smiled at him and suggested. "They will love you for that. Men don't like to shop. It's a good thing you're their boss or they'd have a fit," she laughed. She walked over to the other two women and told them their plans for the next day. Hazel was worried about the work that had stacked up that afternoon but Bertha told her not to worry; she would help her get caught up.

They went back to the office. Bert and Hazel retired to Hazel's office for the rest of the day and at six o'clock, they came down and found Kurt and Eric waiting to escort Bertha home.

Chapter Forty-five

It was rehearsal day and Bert was starting to get nervous. She and Eric went into town earlier in the day and met his staff members from around the states that would be attending the wedding. Bert was impressed at the quality of people Eric had managed to hire at his other eleven offices. One manager could not make it. His wife was expecting their first child the day of the wedding.

Eric got up before the group and announced. "I want to thank you all for clearing your calendars for the next two weeks. I knew that if I told you I needed you here for two weeks, you would be here. Let me explain why I insisted on two weeks.

First I knew you would not take the time off to entertain your wives for two straight weeks." The wives nodded their heads and the men laughed.

"Well now you have too, it's an order," he paused and enjoyed the happy looks on their spouse's faces.

"Next, Hazel will hand out an itinerary for you to follow. She has worked diligently on it so please follow it the first week but feel free to change it the second week if you want, just don't forget, you're on vacation. You all have expense accounts. Your living and sleeping arrangements are on the company but please go a little easy on the Old Man. The first week, the four six passenger company cars will take you to Dearborn to the Ford Museum and Greenfield Village, where you will spend the night and most of the next day. Hazel will give you all your passes. Then you will have a tour of Plymouth and its surrounding areas where you will stay over night before heading north again. Your next stop will be Birch Run to see Bonners Christmas Village. A Christmas display that surpasses anything I have ever seen. You will receive gift certificates you can use there. Back to Gaylord for a day of rest before you will go to Mackinaw Island, a real must see. Again, Hazel will have all the tickets you will need that day. Bertha's friend will meet you at the ferry and show you the Island that few get in to visit. Then on to Sault Saint Marie for a little gambling, for those inclined, and a tour through the Locks for those who aren't." he smiled.

"When you return to Gaylord, Hazel will spend a day familiarizing you with our lovely area."

They all noted he used the term our, it was the first time they had heard their boss use the possessive expression. They were happy he had finely found a place to land. Since most of them started working for the company, He had hopped from state to state and they never knew when or where he would pop up next.

"The remainder of your time the company cars are at your disposal. They will be four in front of the motel for your use. Hazel can suggest some sights of interest but you do as you please until the plane leaves on the seventeenth. Don't think your boss is getting senile. I need a manager up here and if after your stay you decide you'd like to take a crack at it, call or fax me. Now please relax, enjoy yourselves and I order you to have a good time."

The managers and their spouses all stood as one, and applauded Eric. Eric then introduced each one of them personally to Bertha. After everyone had met her and congratulated the new couple, they excused themselves and allowed Hazel to take over the meeting. Hazel would see they arrived the next day at the church and to the reception afterward.

Chapter Forty-six

Eric and Bertha were headed for the rehearsal. They entered the car before raising the garage door, as was their habit of late. He started the car, raised the door and saw Art in the rearview window. Gunning the car into reverse, he hit Art in his right side. Art got up and leaped on a motorcycle he had parked and running in the front drive. Before Eric could warn Bertha to get out of the car and back into the house, Art was out of sight. He hit the panic button on his key chain and heard it blast off and on. "Get in the house honey," he told Bertha. "Lock up and put on the security system. I'm going to use the cell phone and get Kurt back here." He was disgusted with himself for telling Kurt to go in early. He had been selfish, wanting an hour alone with Bertha. That will not happen again, he assured himself. He was going to have to be more careful with his soon to be bride.

Kurt came tearing up the road and into Bertha's driveway. He leaped from his car and shouted. "Which way did that lousy skunk go?"

"I think he is long gone but I have the police on their way. I want you in the house with Bertha until they get here. She is in there alone and I want to stay out here and make sure he doesn't return. I don't think he will; I hit him pretty good with the rear of the car. He has to be hurt."

"Good for you boss," Kurt said and went over to the back door. "Mrs. Schlinkenmayer its Kurt. Let me in please." Nothing happened and he repeated his plea.

"She must be finally listening to me. I told her not to let anyone in unless I told her personally," he smiled, walked over to the door and called her name. She opened the door immediately. "I want Kurt to stay with you until we can leave for the rehearsal," he said.

Kurt entered the house as the chief of police arrived with two squad cars. Eric invited them into the house and they all took seats in the living room and immediately started talking. The men in uniform sat in the living room bay window area. If he was outside lurking, Gary wanted to make sure Art knew his men were there. Eric quickly went over what had just happened and said, "I'm sure the devil is hurt. I hit him pretty good and he was limping seriously when he got on the bike. He won't get too far before he is going to need medical attention."

"Maybe his sister will help us find him. She is the local E.R. head nurse and has nothing to do with her brother. She stopped talking to him after he brought his wife in with a broken arm. She said she knew Nancy didn't just fall in the kitchen as Art insisted. If he comes to her for help, I think she will call us," Gary said. "Let's see you get to the rehearsal safely. I have men on all the roads out of Michaywe and others checking any side roads. They will turn up something soon, if he is hurt. I'll go to the hospital and talk to his sister right after you get settled at the rehearsal dinner." As they were leaving, Gary got another call. He turned and said to Eric, "They found his bike. It was lying in tall grass off on one of the side road. I think you were right, Eric. There was blood on the right side of the bike. He must be pretty badly hurt. How he managed to stay on the bike that far is a miracle. We'll get him now."

Bertha was glad Max, Elizabeth and the babies were not going to be there until after the rehearsal. Max had wanted a few days off so he had to work that day and could not get away before three. Elizabeth would still be able to stand up with her mother and promised to be there in time for the rehearsal dinner. Eric's parents had arrived the previous month. They were settled in at the rental Bertha had found for them. Bert and Eric saw them every day for the past week as the newlyweds were leaving right after the ceremony and would not be back for a month. Bertha made arrangements for Elizabeth and her family to stay in town at the motel where Bertha's sister and brother-in-law-law were staying. Her brother and sister-in-law from Arizona would be at the same motel later that evening. She did not want any of her family in danger and said as much to Eric.

"I agree dear. Hazel has offered her place. I didn't know how well Elizabeth would like it so I convinced her she should be near her aunt and uncle. I think she will be safer there. Gary will have men posted at the motel and the church.

Maybe they will have the skunk by tomorrow," He smiled that smile at her and she felt a warm glow go through her body, erasing the tension that had been building up all day.

"Let's not let him spoil our day," she said.

"We won't dear," Eric assured her.

They arrived at the church and Gary said his men found out Lizzie Plant was not working today. He was going to her house and would not leave until he had searched it thoroughly.

The rehearsal went smoothly and as they were about to leave, Elizabeth and Max arrived with their babies. Hugs were given all around and they all left for the dinner.

They had decided the safest place for the rehearsal dinner was at Bertha's home so she had given a key to Kim and she was to have the meal set up by the time they returned. It was to be a buffet. Everyone could take what he or she wanted and eat at any of the tables set up in the dining room and Bert's office. Kim had the T.V. trays set around the living room if anyone wanted to use an easy chair. They had out done themselves. It could not have been nicer. Kim's mother had made three different salads, bean, spinach, and cucumber. They had cheeses, little egg rolls and spinach roll-ups, before serving the main course of prime rib and salmon, along with a number of side dishes followed by a lovely desert. Everyone ate until they couldn't hold any more food. Kim and two of the server's came in, cleared everything up, and left feeling very proud after the comments made about the excellent feast. They all retired early and Eric said he would sleep in the lower level and not come near the upstairs until after the wedding. Bertha laughed and said he could come for breakfast but he said he wanted this ceremony to be by the book.

Kurt stayed in the guestroom and got little sleep. He had both ears listening for any strange noise. Bert's furnace decided tonight was the night it would do its little squeaky noises again. She had a new fan put in two years ago but it sounded like it would have to be replaced again. About two o'clock Bert ran into Kurt in the kitchen while she was getting a drink of water.

He looked around the corner and said, "I'm sorry, I heard a noise and thought I better check. By the way, this house makes some very funny noises. It took me until one o'clock to trace the worst one to your furnace."

Bert smiled and told him about the fan. "I hope you can get some sleep now. I won't get up again until morning," she told him and went back to her room.

Chapter Forty-seven

August forth arrived clear and bright. The sun shone through the blue spruce trees in her yard and made them shine their most vibrant hue. She loved blue spruce and when she had them planted around the exterior of the house in the front and in the back, everyone teased her as she already had over a hundred trees in her yard. Bertha smiled in the mirror at her reflection. She looked happier than she had in a long time. Even with Art on the loose, she was going to enjoy today and later a month with her Eric. All her worries about their age difference seemed so silly to her now. She went in and showered, got into a housecoat and went to the kitchen to start a pot of coffee. She was so excited and nervous she did not think she could keep anything down but a little coffee. What was the matter with her, she wondered? She had not been this nervous with her first wedding and she was years younger. Maybe that's it; I'm a lot older. She laughed.

Kurt walked into the kitchen. He was completely dressed and his hair was still wet from the shower. "What are you laughing about?" he asked.

"Oh! You wouldn't understand; just bride jitters," she told him and smiled. "Will you take Eric some coffee and rolls? I have them ready to take down but promised I wouldn't see him until the wedding."

"Sure, but don't go anywhere until I get back," Kurt told her. "I'm to drive you to the church and stay with you until Eric can take over."

"I promise sir. I won't leave the house without you and Little Roger," She told him. She knew he called his new revolver, Little Roger. He said it was so he did not have to tell anyone he was packing heat; he would just say he was bringing Little Roger.

Bertha puttered around her house until Annette called to tell her she would be in town the next few weeks and would check the house and water her plants. She wanted to know if there was anything else Bert needed. "No thanks. I'm just killing time, until Kurt takes me to the church. I'll be getting dressed in a few minutes and we'll be taking off. I'll see you there." Bertha told her and went into her bathroom to put on her make-up. For her wedding ensemble, she had chosen a lime green skirt that fell just above the tops of her shoes, with a matching short jacket that buttoned down the front and stopped just before the jacket touched her hips. She bought shoes, and had them dyed to match her outfit. It would double as her going-away attire because she had purchased a matching shorter skirt to wear during the day. The two blouses, one in white and the other lime green would double her wardrobe on her honeymoon. She was going to wear a lime-green hat with a soft brim and small feather in the matching band for her wedding but would leave it behind after the ceremony. Eric told her to pack light and she would not need a hat. He still refused to tell her where they were going. She looked at the time and decided she had better get dressed; she certainly did not want to be late.

She walked out of the room and was met my Kurt. He was wearing a very fashionable, dark gray dress suit and a matching tie with a light gray shirt. "My, I've never seen you so dashing," she smiled. "You look pretty great all cleaned up."

He smiled and said, "Thank you, I'll take that as a compliment. You ready to go and take the big step?"

"As ready as I'll ever be. I didn't think I'd see the day I'd marry again but I think Eric chased me until I caught him," Bert laughed.

"Don't kid yourself," Kurt said. "He was after you from the first day he met you. We ran into one another when he returned to California from his trip back east and he told me he had met the woman he was going to marry. All he had to do was convince her, and we know how convincing old Eric can be," he smiled. "Come on; let's get you to the church before you change your mind."

Kurt checked the car, garage and outside before he allowed Bert to come out. He seated her in the passenger seat, went around the car, and got behind the wheel. When they left the house, Kurt told Bert that the search of Art's sister's house did not produce any clues.

It was a short trip to the church and they were there in five minutes. When they arrived, the minister was waiting and took her into her office. Elizabeth and her other bridesmaids, Eric's sister and Bert's sister were already there. "We thought you might have gotten cold feet," her sister said.

"Why does everyone think I'll get cold feet?" she laughed.

"We were hoping you wouldn't come to your senses until after you married my brother," Mary laughed.

Everyone was in a happy mood. It was going to be a joyous day.

Elizabeth walked over to her mother and buzzed her cheek. "You look lovely, mother. Where did you find that beautiful outfit?"

"I had a local seamstress make it. She made me come in six times to make sure it fit perfectly. I think she did a tremendous job, don't you?"

"I want her name," Hattie said. "It is exquisite. You sure know how to wear clothes. I wonder if she tried real hard she could make me look as good."

They followed each other upstairs to the classrooms so they would have enough room to get ready.

Everyone was ready for the wedding. The church decorated and bride and bridesmaid were getting nervous. The minister was in her white robe and the organist was ready to begin. Mary, the minister came up the stairs and told them everyone had arrived and the men were waiting.

All of a sudden, Bertha felt faint. "Mother, stop it. You look like your ready to faint. You can handle this, if you really want him. He is getting the best deal and we both know it but I think he is also pretty special. Now do you want to go through with this or not?" Bertha nodded her head and smiled. "Then let's get this show on the road." She kissed her mother for the sixth time since she arrived. "You're doing the right thing Mom. Dad would want you to remarry and be happy. You are too good a wife material not to share." She dabbed the tears from Bertha's eyes. "Stop that or you'll spoil both of our make-up. I'm not going to stand up there next to you and have eye make-up running down my cheeks."

Bertha smiled, squeezed her daughter's hand and followed her matron-of-honor from the room.

The music began and as she started down the aisle, she saw Eric at the end, grinning from ear to ear. He has such a wonderful smile, she thought for the hundredth time. She knew when she looked in his eyes she was doing the right thing. She could not see or hear anything but Mary and Eric. She was surprised she had the presence of mind to say, "I do" at the proper time. Mary was pronouncing them man and wife when she realized Eric was about to kiss her. A sweeter kiss she could not remember. She smiled up at him and he had tears in his eyes. Bertha also had happy tears in her eyes.

"Thank you, Schlick you've made me very happy. I'll love you forever and I'll always be there for you."

They turned to walk back up the aisle. It was the first time Bertha noticed the church was packed with friends and relatives. If she had known they were all there she probably would have fainted. Right now, she felt she was ten feet off the ground. They went out to the fellowship hall and stood with her bridesmaids and matron-of-honor in the reception line.

At the reception his staff walked up to the head table and said, "Boss we know you asked for all gifts to be donations to our favorite charities but we had to give you at least one gift." He handed a tall box to Eric and he and Bertha opened it. A large statue of a strong man, with his arms showing how powerful he was; on the bottom was engraved, 'I'm the luckiest man alive, I got Schlick'.

"This is great", he acknowledged, holding it up for all to see and read the engraving. Everyone laughed. They had a gift for Bertha also. It was a golden horseshoe with their names hammered on it. They said being married to him she would need it. It was to hang above the door of their new home. Bert and Eric looked at one another and they both were thinking how they needed all the luck they could get to keep Art out of their lives

. Elizabeth and Max arrived back at the church in time to take their minds back to their own wedding.

Eric was as excited as Bertha when Elizabeth and Max came in carrying the twins. Bertha hired a nurse to be at the reception to care for the twins, but she had little work for the first hour after their arrival because Eric took one twin and Bertha took the other and showed them to each guest.

Eric would say, "Have you met my grandsons," and smiled that smile. "They had to see grandma and grandpa get married properly today."

Bertha thought he was as proud of them as she was. When they started to fuss, Elizabeth took over and went outside the hall to a small room where she could nurse them in private. When they were both fed, she handed them back over to the nurse who put them to bed in the baskets Max had carried in. Max placed the baskets in one corner of the reception area where the nurse could keep an eye on them.

The reception lasted until late that evening. When the limo picked Bert and Eric up to take them to the airport it was well past twelve. They sat so close to each other they looked like one person. They took the confetti out of each other's hair and laughed all the way to their destination. Eric's pilot was waiting and he escorted them aboard. The pilot had left the reception early to take their luggage to the plane and see that everything was in readiness for the newlyweds. They took off shortly after one o'clock and it was the first time Bertha felt the fatigue taking over her body. "Tired darling, sit back and relax," Eric told her.

"You must be tired too," Bertha smiled.

"Yes, I guess I am. Why don't we try to get a few hours sleep, we are five hours or better from L.A. where we will refuel and then several more hours to our destination," He told her. They leaned back in their chairs and held hands. She was about to ask him where but thought better of it. She knew it would be wonderful. She closed her eyes and was asleep within minutes.

When she awoke, Eric was sitting up looking at her. "Do I smell coffee?" she asked.

"Right here, we just made you a pot of decaf. Would you like a roll or one of the sandwiches from last night?" Eric asked.

"No, I think coffee is enough. I'm still stuffed. What time is it?" she inquired.

"Almost morning," he told her. "You were really tired. I only woke up a little while ago."

"I'm sorry dear. I didn't mean to fall asleep."

"We refueled in California and are heading out across the ocean," Eric smiled. "Tom said he should be landing in about four hours. We had a good tail wind and we're making wonderful time. You might want to get some more rest. We will be very busy the next few weeks." He was really getting a kick out of keeping their destination a secret from her.

She looked up at him and smiled, "When are you going to tell me where we are going?" she asked.

"In about four hours," he smiled that smile at her.

Chapter Forty-eight

Arriving at the big Island of Hawaii, Eric thanked his pilot, Tom and helped the driver put their belongings in a limo parked at the curb waiting for them. The limo driver drove directly to the pier were a launch picked them up and deposited them on one of the largest yachts Bertha had ever seen. "I rented it for a month and when we see something we want to stop and look at, we can go ashore. Art won't get at my love here," he smiled.

"I can't believe you rented it for a month. Darling, can we afford such luxury. You only purchased the house last month and with the gifts you're giving the staff, you might get short. I don't need all this, I have you," she smiled at her new husband.

He smiled in return, "Honey I'll buy you this boat if you want it. Now stop worrying we have plenty and as for the staff, that is probably the smartest money the company has ever spent. Not only do rested execs work better and longer hours, but also I'll bet I have at least four transfer letters requesting the Michigan district on my desk by the time we return. Now, no more shop talk. Let's get ready for dinner. The captain has the best chef in the business. That is why I picked the Maryanne.

The newlyweds went down to their stateroom and Bertha unpacked her clothes, placing them in the right hand drawers of the wall length dresser. Eric followed suit and placed his in the left-hand drawers. "See, we even work well on domestics together," he laughed.

"I'll hold my judgment until I see how well you do dishes," She teased.

They changed clothes and then went up on top to the dining room. The chef was excellent. The roast was done to perfection and the veggies were cooked, 'al dente' and were delicious.

After dinner, they enjoyed watching the stars, while seated side by side in deck chairs. When Bertha felt chilly, she got up from her chair and Eric rose and walked over to her. Well Mrs. Hoffermeister how does it feel to be married to a grandpa?" he asked.

"Probably like it does for you to be married to a grandma," she laughed.

"It feels wonderful to me. I get a bride I been looking for years to find, in the bargain," he said and took her in his arms, kissing her tenderly. Their passion was beginning to get to both of them and he suggested, "Shall we call it a day?"

"Let's; I'd like the privacy of our room," she said and they left the deck.

Once in the room, Bertha went into the small changing area and put on her new lingerie. She had chosen a lace pink nightgown with a pink silk robe. Of course, she wore matching slippers. She appeared in the doorway and Eric was in white satin pajama bottoms. He took a deep breath and walked slowly over to her.

"I want to please you so," he said. "I'll take it slow and easy. I know this isn't easy for you, but know I love you deeply."

"I love you too darling and I could not be happier. Kiss me before I die from waiting," she smiled tenderly up at him.

He bent down and kissed her and they moved slowly over to the large bed.

In the middle of the night, Bertha sat up in bed. "That's it," she cried.

Eric awoke with a start. "What is it, dear? Are you all right?" he cried.

"Yes dear. I just figured out where that skunk is hiding," she said.

"Where? Tell me. I'll call Kurt right away and he can check it out," Eric told her.

"He is in the crawl space beneath the stairwell," Bert told him.

"What crawl space. Honey you're not making sense. There is no crawl space in your home," Eric insisted.

"Yes there is. You enter it through the cedar closet. There is an access door to the pipes for the downstairs sink and drain. He isn't at our place; he's at Lizzy's. Do you remember we both thought my clothes, the day someone broke into my home, smelled of cedar even though I had removed the clothes days before and aired them before I wore them? It wasn't me; it was Art. He had been in my home. Lizzy must have built a

cedar closet in her lower level just like mine," she said
.   "How do you know? The police didn't mention it or the access door," Eric said.

"Yes they did. When the chief said they checked the house from top to bottom including the attic and closets," Bertha said.

"Yes, I remember him saying that," Eric said. "I suppose he could have meant a cedar closet.

"While you were in your office last week, I spoke to one of the officers the chief had watching us," Bertha told him.

"Go on dear," Eric said.

"He said he purchased a real bargain that week. He said he was going to build a sauna and when he went to the lumber company, they said Lizzy had ordered too much wood for a cedar closet she was installing in her basement, and insisted they sell the excess to someone else. The man at the lumberyard said he has had it lying around for several weeks and wanted to get rid of it; so the officer got it real cheap. Don't you see; she has a very similar floor plan as mine, with the stairway off the main entrance, leading to her lower level. If she built the cedar closet next to that stairway, where I have mine, it would be real easy to hide a small door going to the space under the stairs. The chief even said they had searched the closets. That has to be where he is. He needed medical attention and his sister is a nurse and has access to any bandages or drugs he might need. Where else could he be," she said excitedly. "He hasn't shown up at any hospitals and we both know he was hurt bad."

He gave her a big hug. "I think you might have solved his disappearance, honey. I'll call Kurt right away and he can get a hold of the chief of police. They can run out there. Where will they find the access door do you think?" he said.

"Probably, behind some shelves or something, on the wall facing the door as you walk into the closet. That is a perfect place for it to allow you entree under the staircase," She smiled. "We got him honey; I know we've found him."

Eric smiled and got on his cell phone. He was surprised it worked. They must have arrived at the first Island while they slept. He called Kurt and he answered the phone on the first ring. "Don't you ever sleep man?" Eric asked.

"Eric, what is it. Is everything all right?" he questioned back. "It's the middle of the night here."

"We couldn't be better. Listen carefully. Bertha thinks she knows where our skunk is hiding and I think she is right. I want you to wake Gary, get a search warrant and get him out to Lizzy's right away," he said and repeated all that Bertha just told him.

"I'll bet you're right. I'll get on it right away. I sure hope you are. I'll enjoy disturbing Art's sleep. Can I get you by cell phone to let you know if all went well?" Kurt asked.

"Yes! I'll leave it on. Thanks Kurt, I appreciate all you're doing for us," Eric told him.

"Stop talking like that. I'd do it even if I wasn't getting paid," he laughed. "But don't get any ideas," Kurt said and disconnected.

"Well darling all we can do now is to wait. Let's try to get some sleep or----something," he said, rolling over, he took her in his arms.

Chapter Forty-nine

Bertha and Eric were leaving for breakfast when his cell phone went off. He picked it up and answered it. When he heard Kurt's voice he said, "Just a minute, I want Schlick to hear this." He put his head set into his phone and handed her half of it. They put their heads together and both listened. "Go ahead pal."

Kurt was excited. "We got him Bert. He was right where you said he'd be. He is hurt pretty bad and running a fever but the chief won't let him go to the hospital. He put him in jail and has the doctor and nurses attending him there. They had to re-set his ankle and I don't think they were too tender about it. The chief made them do it in his cell. He said there is no way he will get out of his custody. He is going to give him over to the California police if they have a strong enough case. The California police are flying in to discuss it with him. If they don't, the chief said at least he could get him for the attempted murder of a private detective. Art is still not talking, but he will, or I'll personally break his other ankle. Too bad, they don't hang guys anymore. Oh! The chief wants me to thank Bertha personally. You are quite a lady," He said. "Enough of the ugly stuff my best friends. Have a lovely honeymoon and rest easy. Everything here is under control. We will see you when we see you," he concluded.

"Thanks pal, I owe you," Eric said.

"Yes Kurt, thank you," Bertha said.

"Happy to be of service; see you soon," Kurt said and then rang off.

Eric hugged his new wife and told her, "You're safe now honey. What would you like to do today? He asked. "We can go anywhere and do anything that pleases you."

"I am so happy right now; I don't care what we do. I think we should inspect the Island, buy the twins some things and do a little shopping after a long slow breakfast," she suggested.

"Sounds perfect. Let's go to breakfast," he leered at her and took her in his arms again. "On second thought maybe it's a little early for breakfast," He smiled.

Around an hour later, Eric took Bertha's hand and led her out on deck to go to their waiting meal.

Chapter Fifty

Traveling among the Islands, Bert and Eric enjoyed every minute of the trip up until now. They had a pile of souvenirs and gifts for everyone. They tried to purchase something on each Island. It was great fun for a couple weeks but Eric started looking a little bored. Bert had to admit she was also getting fidgety. When they awoke that morning she said, "Honey, shall we head for home? I don't know about you; it has been wonderful but I would like to get on dry land. I sway when I walk." She smiled at him.

He smiled back down on her. She had her head on his chest and he was holding her so he could kiss the back of her ear. "You really know me. I am ready to go home if you are. Like you said, it has been wonderful but enough is enough. I have never been away from work this long in my life. I guess I stretched our honeymoon a little too long."

"Never!" she said. "It has been delightful. We have been to places I would never have been able to go before marrying you. The things we have done and people we have met will remain in our memories forever. Neither of us have been seasick a day and we have seen some rough weather. The patches the doctor gave us for behind our ear have worked as advertised. I don't know how any honeymoon could have been more perfect," She looked back over her left shoulder and he planted a big kiss on her lips.

They were up on deck less than an hour later eating at their breakfast table when the captain came in and Eric suggested they look for dry land. He told him he would pay for the month, but they thought they would like to start for home.

"We can continue on this course for a couple days and be at Catalina Island, California by the end of the week. That is my next tour stop. You will only miss a week and I will be where I have to be for the next group. We'll call it even. You'll not have to pay for the last week and I will not lose a week if I dropped you off in Hawaii," He said.

Bertha smiled. That was the most conversation the captain and Eric had in the weeks they had been on board. The crew and captain had been wonderful. They stayed out of their way and were there only if Bertha or Eric needed something. The two men agreed and the Captain headed for the pilothouse.

Eric and Bertha went up on deck to sit in their deck chairs. Closing their eyes, they allowed the sun to wash over them. Bertha opened her swimsuit coverall, and her lovely new pink suit showed where her old tan lines were. Eric had purchased it at the last stop and she wore it this morning because she knew it would please him. It was a little more revealing than she would have purchased for herself. He smiled over at her and said, "That suit does wonders for you." He grinned, "It does wonders for me too."

"Behave your-self," she teased and took his hand. They sat holding hands for a long time.

Chapter Fifty-one

The yacht pulled into Catalina Harbor on Friday and a limo was at the dock waiting for the Hoffermeister couple. Eric handed an envelope to each crewmember and shook their hands, thanking them for their efforts. He went over to the Captain and did the same. The crew stood on deck and saluted as they went down the gangplank.

When they got to the limo they found their luggage and packages had already been put in the trunk and part of the passenger area. Eric held the door for Bertha and then crawled in next to her. He put his arm around her and said. "I rented us a room at the Ritz in Laguna Hills. I thought you might like to spend a little time there and have our friends and family join us."

"Oh, honey, what a splendid idea. Did you call mother Hoffermeister?" she asked.

"Yes, but you better call her, Hattie," he smiled. "She wanted to come today but I asked her to wait a day. I didn't know what time we would be arriving. I rented several rooms on the same floor so my folks and any of your friends that want to stay overnight can be near us."

They arrived at the Ritz and were shown to a lovely suite. When they walked into the room, they saw a large fruit bowl, a bottle of champagne, smoked oysters, cheeses and crackers lay out on a small side table. Eric insisted on carrying her over the threshold. He said it was not the same as carrying her into a stateroom on the ship. He placed her down on the floor and walked over to pour them both a glass of champagne. "Is this the Honeymoon Suite?" she asked.

"Of course! Do you like it?" he asked.

"Lovely, but I think they probably will wonder about us. We are a little long in the tooth to be newlyweds," she smiled, "but I must admit, I've never felt younger," she told him. She accepted the glass and gave him a buzz on the cheek.

"I can't believe you have ever been more lovely," He said and put his arm around her.

"Talk like that will get you anything," she smiled.

They rested until dinner and had it served in their room. They did not want to have everyone know who the newlyweds were and wanted to enjoy each other's company.

The next day Hattie and Budd arrived. Mary and Steve had flown out a week earlier and rode over with Eric's parents. They had a small family reunion and dined later that afternoon, joined by three couples Bertha used to live near. She introduced Eric to them and they enjoyed a wonderful luncheon Eric had planned.

Her friends did not stay that evening but Eric's family planned to spend a couple days. He arranged several side trips to places of interest. He must have spent hours planning, as each time they went to a restaurant, the hostess was waiting for them. They spent three terrific days there and then Eric and Bertha flew home.

Chapter Fifty-two

Eric and Bertha drove up to Eric's new home and the limo driver helped Eric carry their belongings up onto the porch, but not before Eric carried Bertha over the threshold, again. When he placed her down on the floor, she smiled and said, "I hope that is the last time you have to strain your back carrying me over a threshold."

"If I wasn't busy, I'd carry you around all day," he smiled that smile and kissed her before going back out to retrieve the rest of the luggage.

They were not fully unpacked when the phone started ringing. Eric answered to hear his friend Kurt on the other end of the line. "Sure Kurt, come on over," he said and hung up the phone. "Kurt is on his way over. He wants to tell us the latest," he told her.

"I'll put a pot of coffee on. I'm afraid we don't have anything in the house to go with it," Bertha told him.

"Honey, don't worry about it," He said, giving her a peck on the cheek. "We will go to the grocery tomorrow. We can have dinner at the club tonight."

Kurt arrived ten minutes later. Accepting the coffee Bertha offered he took a seat in the living room. "You both look rested. How was the cruise?" he asked.

Bertha knew he was just trying to be polite. He really wanted to get down to the case. "It could not have been better, thank you," Bertha told him. "How were things back here?"

"Yes, Is he still in the local jail or did California take him?" Eric asked.

"We had him up until yesterday. He won't talk to anyone. He was arraigned here and California took precedence over him so we gave them first crack at him. If they can't pin murder on him; we get him back." Kurt said. "I'm glad you got back early. I'll be taking a vacation for a few weeks, if you can spare me. I want to go out there and make sure they don't mess up again."

"I want you to go but you don't need to take your vacation time. I might join you later when he goes to trial," Eric said.

"Not without your partner," Bertha interrupted
.

Eric smiled at his wife seated next to him, put his arm around her and said, "I wouldn't think of going without you."

The doorbell rang and Eric went to answer it. "He keeps saying he isn't guilty," Kurt told Bertha as she waited to see who was at the door.

"Of course he would say that. How many murderers admit they killed their victim?" Bertha said.

"You have a point. I think he is guilty of something but something about this case smells.

I want to go and make sure he hasn't paid someone to get him off out there. He still has contacts on the force." Kurt informed her.

Eric and Gary walked into the living room. "Chief Gary, how nice to see you. May I get you a cup of coffee?" Bertha said.

"Thank you Bertha that would be very nice," Gary told her.

"Get the coffee honey and then Gary wants to talk to both of us," Eric told her

.   Bert brought the coffee into the chief and sat it on the table next to his chair.

"Go ahead chief. Schlick, sit here next to me," Eric said and patted the seat next to him. She went over and sat as close to him as possible. She had a premonition she was not going to like this conversation.

"Well, as Kurt probably already told you, we had Art but gave him up to the L.A. police. They took him back to California and locked him in maximum security. They have been interrogating him since they got him but are not getting anymore out of him than we did. He still insists he's innocence," he said.

"So, what else is new," Kurt murmured. "They knew he would never admit to a crime of murder. He's nuts but not that nuts."

"Yeah!" the chief said, "but he insists he will talk; if we bring him the right person to tell his story too."

"Who could get him to talk?" Eric asked, and when he saw the chief look over at Bert he said, "No! I will not submit Bertha to that swine. He just wants to try and get his hands on her.

You're asking us to put her in the same room with that clown?" he bellowed.

"Calm down honey. No one is going to put me in peril," Bert said. "There will be police with me in the room and a window between me and Art; right chief?"

"Yes Ma'am and I'll be one of them in the room at all times," Gary said.

"You're actually thinking of going out there?" Eric said squeezing her hand.

"Honey, if it takes that to get him to confess, I don't mind," Bert said.

"Okay, Gary. We will both go to L.A. and see our man," Eric said.

"I'll set it up. The company jet is in for its yearly maintenance check up," Gary told him and went over to the phone. "Probably next Wednesday. That will give them a few more days to see if they can get him to confess without getting Bertha involved anymore then she has been."

After Gary left, Kurt said, "I've got reservations but they are for Monday. I'll call and let you two know if they found out anything. I'll let you get some rest now. You had a long trip today."

"You have to eat. Why don't you join us at the clubhouse around six thirty," Eric told him.

"I don't want to interfere with the newlyweds," Kurt smiled.

"We have to start seeing people eventually," Bert laughed.

They agreed to meet at the clubhouse and Bertha went into the bedroom and started unpacking. She left an empty suitcase lay open on the cedar chest so later that evening she could start packing for their trip out west.

Chapter Fifty-three

Wednesday, Bert walked into the room they had set aside for the interview. Two uniformed police officers and Gary followed her. They seated her on one side of a long table with a twenty-inch high piece of glass running down the middle. They waited only seconds when a shackled Art walked into the room. He smiled his sick smile when he saw Bertha seated at the table and sat in a chair on the other side of the glass.

"How nice you came to visit me," he said.

"This is not a social call Art and you know it. They said you wanted to talk to me," Bertha said

.   "You better be nicer to me, or I won't tell you anything either," He said. It was obvious he was not playing with a full deck. He had finally gone off the deep end.

"All right Art. Tell me what you think I should know?" Bert said.

"First, I didn't kill anyone. I swear I'm no killer." Art said.

"Which murder are we talking about?" Bert asked. She was hoping he was relaxing and would start revealing more.

He loved to brag and he made up his mind he wanted Bertha to believe what a big man he was, and how he could talk anyone into anything.

"Let's start with Nancy. Ugh! I could never slit anybody's throat. We had our problems but I couldn't do her in the way she was killed." His eyes actually started to tear up but only a little. "My other wives were okay but Nancy was the best."

"Why did you beat her than?" Bertha asked.

"I never laid a hand on her; I swear," Art said.

It had been two hours since she came into the room and Bertha was beginning to get irritated. She had seen Nancy too many times with bruises and he still said he never laid a glove on any of his wives. He was either a good liar or he really did not believe he killed his wives. He even had Bert beginning to have doubts. She told him she had to leave for a few minutes. "If you'll excuse me Arthur, I'll be right back."

"Sure, take your time. I'm not going anywhere," he laughed.

She walked out of the room and into the room with the two-way mirror. Kurt, Detective Sinclair and Eric were waiting. "What do you think?" Bert asked Eric.

"I don't know," he told her.

"Well! I'm having doubts. Did you hear, when I kept asking him about the beatings?" she asked. "He was adamant he had not touched her."

"Yeah! Well, I know one way to see if he is lying, Detective Sinclair," Kurt said turning to the

L.A. officer. "How about giving him a lie detector test, if he will submit to one. It won't be perfect but at the least we will know if our hunch is right."

Detective Sinclair looked at Bertha and said, "Mrs. Hoffermeister, if you can get him to agree; I'll have a test set up immediately. His attorney has been asking for one and we have been avoiding it. If he is telling the truth to you, we have our work cut out for us. I thought we were almost ready to go to trial."

"I have a feeling that is what he and the killer wanted," Kurt frowned. "If we took him to trial without his confession there is a chance he might walk. I've said all along there has to be a reason he wanted to be sent to California."

All this time Gary had come out of the interview room and was standing in the shadows of the tiny room. He stepped forward and said, "Bertha is a good judge of character and I would go with her hunches any day."

"That's good enough for me," the detective said and they watched while Bertha went back into the interview room. As soon as he heard Art agreeing to the test, he left and came back ten minutes later with a young technician and his equipment. They went directly into the room with Bertha and Art.

"I'll leave and," Bertha started to say, but Art interrupted her.

"No! I want you in here. I want to prove to you I am not the monster you think I am," Art said.

Bertha thought to herself. Oh, of course you're not crazy. I wonder who it was that tried to kill my Eric. However, she held her tongue and sat back down.

The detective nodded for her to have a seat so Art could see her and told the tech to start his equipment as it took a while to set up and said to Art, "Your attorney has agreed to it and should be here any moment."

"I don't need him. Bertha won't let you bully me," He said and looked over to her for support. It was all she could do to smile back at him.

Art's attorney came in a few minutes later and asked, "She going to set in on this?" He did not acknowledge he knew who she was but she had the feeling no one had to tell him.

"Art insists she stay," Sinclair told him. "We are about to start if you're satisfied."

"Art, are you sure you want to do this. If it goes bad for you, they will want to submit the results in court," his attorney said.

"Yeah, but we will want to use the results at my trial. Cause I didn't do it," Art demanded.

The test was over and the tech left with his equipment. They all knew Art had passed the test, before the technician informed them. They left the room and Art was taken back to his cell.

Bertha went into the tiny room and directly into the arms of Eric. He held her close and whispered in her ear. "It's over darling. We can go home now if you want or we can go see Mom and dad."

"I'd like to see Hattie. She is so easy to talk to. You're wonderful, but she is a woman and will know how I feel right now," Bertha said.

"Tell me dear. I will try to understand," Eric said. They sat and talked for several minutes and then he said, "I didn't realize how hard this was going to be on you. You did a wonderful job. The rest is up to Sinclair and his men. Gary and Kurt are going to hang around for a few days. I think we are probably free to go."

Detective Sinclair walked into the room as he was talking to Bertha and said to Eric, "Actually if you and Mrs. Hoffermeister could stay around for a few days; we would appreciate it. Art seems to open up to Mrs. Hoffermeister when he won't even talk to anyone else but his sister."

"His sister is here?" Bertha inquired. "They didn't hold her for an accessory in Michigan?"

"She was, but she flew back home. Your local police said she has no criminal record and had several people vouch for her honesty. They said that since she had no choice, it was her brother after all and her only living relative. She could not very well turn him down. As much as she hated him, when he came to her and was badly hurt, she said her nursing instincts just took over. She is supposed to return this weekend. She has been trying to get him to confess. I was hoping you might stay until after her next visit. He is always down after talking to her and you may be able to take over where she leaves off," the detective said.

Eric answered, "We will be at my folks; you have the number." He took Bertha's arm and led her from the room and out of the building. He did not say Bertha would or would not return to speak to Art again.

Chapter Fifty-four

Bertha and Eric arrived at his parents home two hours after leaving police headquarters. Eric wanted to check out of their hotel room first and stay with his folks for a few days. He thought Bertha needed the stabilizing factor of his mother and dad's home.

Hattie and Budd met them at the door. Hattie put her arms around Bertha, comforting her and welcomed Bert into her home. She practically fell into her mother in law's arms.

They spent three glorious days with Hattie and Budd. Eric played tennis two days with his father and was happy he won a couple sets. His dad was very good and when Bertha played one game against him she cried, "Uncle! He is too much for me," she laughed. "Hattie can give him a run for his money once in a while; on one of his off days, but she says the same thing."

They were having dinner when Kurt stopped by the house. He was excited and they could see he was bursting with news. They sat in the living room and he started talking. "Art's second lie detector test came out like we expected. He agreed to another after you left and this time we used his lawyer's technician. There is a strong possibility he is not our killer. I have been with him daily and his stories never change. Not like they were rehearsed, but they didn't change." He explained. "His sister is coming tomorrow and the chief would like Bertha to be there. Maybe he will tell her more after Lizzy leaves. We are checking out some of the things we discussed and find we may be on the right track. It would just be a big help and save a lot of man-power hours if you would speak to him again," he finished and looked over at Bert.

"We will be there. I would like to hear what Lizzy says to him. I am surprised she comes to see him. I hope we are all wrong," Bert concluded.

"You don't have to do this Honey, if you don't want to," Eric told Bert.

"No dear. We might as well get it over with. I am tired of thinking about it. It is time we got back to our home and start our new life," she said and leaned into his shoulder.

He hugged her and told Kurt to look for them about an hour before Lizzie was expected.

Eric showed him to the door and went back in to have a second cup of coffee.

They spent a quiet evening at Hattie and Budd's home avoiding the subject of Art. Bert and Eric retired early. It was going to be a long day tomorrow.

Chapter Fifty-five

Bertha, Eric, Gary, Kurt and Sinclair were again seated in the room with the two-way mirror, off the visitor's area, when Lizzie walked into the room. Art, still wearing his manacles, came in two minutes later. There was a table between him and her but no high-glassed runners down the middle.

Their conversation started amicable enough. Lizzy was polite to her brother but he seemed a little distracted. It was as though he did not really care if she came to visit him or not. He was asking her for something and she was refusing. There were several other tables in use in the room so it was difficult to hear all they were saying. She shouted angrily at him and he cowered down in his chair. It looked like she gave him a ten-minute tongue-lashing. He finally put his head down on the table with his arm wrapped around his hair. She slid her hand out of her pocket and placed it under his arm as though trying to get him to raise his head up or had she slipped him something under the arm. She rose and said goodbye. When she left the room, Art raised his head and there were tears running down his face.

"Get in there, quick," the detective said to Bertha and she rose and left the room. By this time everyone else had left the room and she and the two police officers were the only ones present.

She approached Art as he was wiping his face on his sleeve. "Hello! I thought I'd stop in before I return home. My, you look upset. Is anything wrong? Are they man-handling you here?" she asked sympathetically.

"No, it's not them; it's that darned sister of mine. She called me all sorts of names. I should be used to it by now. She has always been mean to me, ever since we were kids. She calls me all sorts of names," he repeated.

"Why would she be like that? What names does she call you?" Bert asked trying to get him to talk.

"She tells me I'm weak and indecisive. She says I can never stand up for myself and without her, I would be nothing. You don't think I'm weak do you? I know you don't," answering his own question. "She profited from their deaths too," Remembering he was talking aloud; he quickly put his hand over his mouth.

"Arthur, whatever is the matter. You can tell me anything. You know that," Bert tried to reassure him. "They are going to try you for the murder in California. Arthur, you are going to jail for life if they don't put you on death-row."

"No, they can't prove anything against me," he sneered.

"Arthur, listen to me. I snooped around and found they have a very strong case against you.

The coroner found traces of a foreign substance in your second wife that killed her."

"Well! She isn't as smart as she thinks she is than is she," he said.

"Who isn't, Arthur?" Bert asked.

"Lizzy, of course. She should have pushed her overboard like she did my first wife. They never found her body, you know," Arthur rambled on. "You don't think I'm unmanly or weak do you?" He asked her again.

"No, of course not. I think your sister talked you into situations you could not get out of. It looks like she wanted to get rich off you," Bert said.

"That's it exactly. She said after she killed Mabel, my first wife; we would be in clover. She took half of what I got and than she really got greedy, when I married my second wife Bernie. Bernie wouldn't let her live with us so she did away with her too," Arthur said.

"Arthur what happened to Nancy?" Bertha asked. His head began to nod, "Come on, and hold your head up. We've gone this far; you may as well finish it."

"She was always slapping Nancy around. I couldn't get her to stop. Nancy and I were both afraid of her. She has a terrible temper. Once when she visited us, she hit Nancy so hard she lost our baby. After she miscarried, the doctor said if she ever got pregnant again she would never carry the baby full term. We quit trying after that but Nancy never got over it. I never should have moved us to Michigan but Lizzy told me my money would be safer there."

"Why?" Bertha asked.

"She said we would put some of it in a joint account and the money we didn't want anyone to know about, we could put it in safety deposit boxes. That way Nancy would never know our net worth. We lived off Nancy's money for a while and for a long time she didn't seem to mind. Not until my sister started getting rough with her," Art began to ramble. "I was sorry to see her die, she was a good woman," he sniveled. You know. I really was away from home when she killed Nancy. I had gone down state to see an attorney about a Trust Fund. Lizzy said it would be a good idea to set it up with an attorney in Lansing. She said if we set up trust funds and made each other as beneficiary no outsider could touch our money," he mumbled something and his head started swaying forward and backward. He looked like he had been drugged. It was the first time Bertha noticed the white powder around his right nostril.

"Arthur, did she give you something. Did you sniff something up your nose?" Bertha asked.

"It's just to help me relax," he said. "She brought it to me so I could get a good nights sleep," and his head fell forward onto the table. He was unconscious.

Bertha looked toward the two-way mirror and yelled, "We need help in here. Get an ambulance."

Both police officers saw her panic and rushed over signaling for the doctor as they ran into the room. The one officer bent down and with his handkerchief, picked up a white packet he found lying at Arthur's feet. The doctor came in and they rushed Art to the hospital.

Chapter Fifty-six

Kurt stayed at the door of Art's room for three days. It took that long for Art to regain consciousness. Kurt said he was there to make sure Art did not walk away from another hospital.

Lizzy had rushed back to Michigan right after seeing Art and before she found out if he was dead or alive. She had put enough drugs in the little packet to overdose a cow, so she was not worried. She knew that sniveling, weak-kneed brother of hers would start snorting the drug as soon as she left. He always needed something whenever things started getting tough for him. At least she would not have to furnish him drugs any longer. She went back to work the next day as if she had never left town.

The L.A. police announced Arthur's death at three fifteen Monday morning from an overdose of barbiturates that had been smuggled into the prison by person or persons unknown. They told the press there was always someone trying to get drugs inside the prison for the inmates.

Bertha and Eric stayed for another week with his parents and then he had his company jet return them to Michigan. On board were Gary,

Kurt and Art. They planned their departure to get them home after dusk. Gary did not want anyone to know they had a very live and angry Arthur on board. As soon as the police showed him the report on the little packet his sister had given him, Art agreed to testify against her. He knew she had tried to kill him. He also realized she had all his money transferred to her account before his death was announced in the papers.

As soon as Art went into the hospital in a coma, Eric had called his office and put Sally and Don Benjamin in charge of keeping an eye on Lizzy. They called and told him that the bank was the first stop she made when she returned to town. Art was very upset with his sister and finally wanted to get back at her.

Gary had two police cars meet them at the airport and He and one officer took charge of the prisoner. Kurt tagged along with the officers and the chief in their car to make sure he saw personally that Art was locked up safe. Bertha and Eric were driven by the other police officer to their home and arrived there shortly after midnight.

Bertha sighed, a very deep sigh, when she entered the house. "Home sweet home," she smiled at Eric. "I don't know when I have been so happy to be home."

"I'm glad you feel that way. I was a little afraid you wouldn't like this place as well as the one you left," he said and kissed her while they stood in the front hall.

"I'm happy wherever you are dear," Bertha told him and they went in to retire for the night.

Chapter Fifty-seven

At her arraignment, Lizzy lost her temper and laughed at the accusations. Her attorney warned her she was not making points with the court. He did not want to represent her, but was appointed by the presiding judge.

Trial was scheduled to take place in three weeks. From the first day of the trial, her attorney tried to get the case thrown out. He said Lizzy was working a twelve-hour shift the day the deceased died and there were a hundred people she had under her direction at the hospital that would testify to the fact. He also hammered home the fact that she was a registered nurse and worked in the surgical ward during many operations. There was no way she would not have made a cleaner incision in the victim. "Her training would have automatically taken over. Nancy Plant must have done it to herself; it was such a sloppy job. This woman is being tried by circumstantial evidence and heresy information. The tapes the prosecution is so proud of could or could not be from her brother. If they were authentic, what condition was Mr. Plant in when they got him to lie on the tape in question? He was heavily sedated and at deaths door. The lie detector tapes should also be thrown out. They were made in another state and are inadmissible if not administered by Michigan experts." He argued, "The local D.A. is looking for someone to hang a crime on that they do not have the ability to solve. This is a professional, dedicated nurse. There is not one person that will not tell you she is one of the best thought of people in the community. I ask again that the court dismiss all charges against my client."

The district attorney rose from his seat and said, "I have heard a bunch of nonsense in court before but my learned opponent just muttered some of the best I've ever had the misfortune to sit through. This woman is a cold-blooded killer. We have testimony from her brother. Witness's to her being away from the hospital on a so-called emergency call for over an hour the day of the murder. Witness's to testify in regard to her vicious temper whenever people don't see things her way. I will match witness for witness on the women's character with the defendant's attorney. I not only want the trial set for this murder but also for the abetting on the attempted murder of Mr. Hoffermeister.

Before he finished the statement the opposing attorney shouted, "I object. She is being tried for one killing, your honor," the defendant's attorney demanded.

"Sorry sir," the D.A. corrected himself. "The murder of Nancy Plant." He smiled at the opposing attorney. "I also want bail set at one million dollars. Miss Plant has too much money hidden away that would allow her to skip the country."

The judge saw the case the D.A's way, and set the bail high enough they all knew Lizzy would not run out on that much money. To everyone's surprise, she did not even try to make bail. She was going to play the injured party. She liked being a martyr. Her friends all flocked around her and wanted her to let them try to make bail for her. She thought she might allow them to try but if they ever found out her real worth, she would be dog meat. She needed all the support she could get. This was going to be a long and costly trial. She would allow them to hold fundraisers to help pay her attorney costs, however. It was as she told her friends and supporters. "The D.A. needs a scapegoat and now that my brother is dead, they had to pin it on someone and who else but an older, single women with no living relatives and too little money to hire a good defense." She even managed a few tears for them.

All witness's and evidence had to be revealed to both attorneys and when Arthur Plants name appeared, Lizzy and her attorney assumed they were talking about Arthur's tapes. Her attorney knew he could place a lot of doubt on the authenticity of the tapes so they were not worried.

It took over a week to seat a jury in place. Everyone seemed to have already formed an opinion of Lizzy, either they were for her or really against her. They went through all the perspective jurors the court would allow. Finally, after seven days they were ready to go to trial.

Bert and Eric sat through all the defense's witnesses and Bert thought of her part in all this mess. "I would have been one of them if this trial had taken place six months earlier. She's fooled so many people. I was one of Lizzy's biggest fans," she told Eric.

He smiled and patted her hand. "She has fooled a lot of people for a lot of years."

The courtroom was packed the day the D.A. called his fifth witness. He had several witnesses' earlier referring to Lizzy as a Jackal and Hyde personality. Each time, receiving an objection from opposing council. When he called witness number five; everyone was a little tired of the proceedings. They didn't seem to be getting anywhere, and the jury looked half-asleep.

"I now call Arthur Plant to the stand," he said. There was a hush over the entire courtroom and then a large gasp as Art walked into the courtroom and directly up to the witness chair.

"I object, your honor. This man was presumed dead. He has no right being here without our prier knowledge," he said.

"Your honor, council has before him a sheet of paper stating Arthur Plants testimony was to be witness number five," the D.A. said.

"You knew the way you worded it, we thought you were referring to tapes," the opposing council said.

"Gentlemen to the bar," the judge said. When they both approached the bar, he stated, "I am going to allow Mr. Plants testimony. I will agree with you the D.A. could have made it clearer that Mr. Plant was not dead and was willing to testify, but Council, it never came up, and the D.A. did notify you who he was going to call for his fifth witness. I see no other way but to allow his testimony."

"I want a mistrial," the attorney said.

"On what grounds? I will however give you a one day recess to regain your composure and go over his expected testimony but that is all I'll give you," the judge stated.

"I'll take it," the defense council angrily answered.

"Court will be recessed until ten o'clock tomorrow morning," the judge announced.

Gary went up to the witness chair and hurried Arthur out of the courthouse.

Bertha and Eric were met outside the courtroom. Along with several friends, and all they wanted to talk about was the case. When they finally got away Eric and Bertha went directly home. After the trial began, they had decided to have their meals at home until the trial was over.

Lizzy made bail that afternoon and was seen heading up north to the nearest large airport. She tried to escape but Gary had been way ahead of her. He had men posted at airports as far south as Detroit and as far north as Marquette. Marquette was where they finally arrested her. She had switched from her car to a bus and was free until one of Gary's men picked her up at the airport. Her hair was cut short, enabling her to wear a blond wig. She wore none of her usual heavy make-up. She had jeans and a matching shirt on and was pretty well disguised.

She was returned and stood trial the following day. The trial did not last long as the defense fell apart after she tried to flee. They heard Arthur Plant's testimony and that sealed the case. All the poor defending council could do was object to any reference to other murders that the D.A.   mentioned. The jury was out for only six hours when they brought back a verdict of guilty of the first-degree murder of Nancy.

Next would be the sentencing and they all felt it would be life. The courtroom was still packed however when the judge gave her life, with no possibility of parole.

Arthur was given a light sentence since he testified against Lizzy, on behalf of his dead wife, Nancy. It was not his fault he was weak and his sister had controlled him since he was a baby. It was amazing the power she had over him. Even at the trial he could not look at her. During his entire testimony, he stared at Eric or Bertha. The only time he looked at his sister was to point her out to the court. He was placed at a prison work camp and was required to see a counselor twice a week for his entire stay. Gary told him it would be good for him to be out in the air. They were all hoping when his five years was up he would have a clear mind and a better attitude on life.

Bert and Eric tried to get back to work but neither of them could concentrate on business. They decided to take a long extended vacation, maybe to Branson. That was the first place they knew for sure, they loved one another.

Eric reached over with his right hand and squeezed hers. They smiled at one another and

Eric drove her little camper out of the driveway.

THE END

WATCH FOR BOOK TWO OF THE BERTHA MYSTERY.